Gunman's Pledge

Infamous gunslinger Wes Longbaugh is heading for his next job in Utah when he comes across a traveller cast afoot in Nevada's arid Humboldt Sink. Never one to turn the other cheek when help is needed, Wes intercepts the staggering loner. It turns out that Mace Farlow was the sole outlaw to survive a stagecoach robbery that had gone badly awry. All the other robbers had been gunned down due to the treachery of a turncoat.

Mace tags along with his saviour but is determined to track down the double-crosser. Fate, however, takes a hand when trouble in the next town leads to flight and a stand-off in a lonely canyon, where Mace is killed. Before he dies, the aging outlaw makes his young sidekick promise to abandon the precarious life of a gunslinger. But this is far harder to achieve than Wes could ever have imagined.

Gunman's Pledge

Ethan Flagg

A Black Horse Western

ROBERT HALE

© Ethan Flagg 2019
First published in Great Britain 2019

ISBN 978-0-7198-2958-1

The Crowood Press
The Stable Block
Crowood Lane
Ramsbury
Marlborough
Wiltshire SN8 2HR

www.bhwesterns.com

Robert Hale is an imprint
of The Crowood Press

Typeset by
Derek Doyle & Associates, Shaw Heath
Printed and bound in Great Britain by
4Bind Ltd, Stevenage, SG1 2XT

ONE

SNAKE IN THE GRASS

'Make sure those logs are laid out across the whole trail.'

Juno Macklin's gruff order was aimed at two hard-faced jaspers while he himself strutted around directing operations. Mace Farlow and his sidekick Whiskey Dan grunted as they trundled the heavy obstructions into place.

Macklin was a dour, grim-faced outlaw boasting a luxuriant black moustache who enjoyed giving orders. It had always been the same since his school days. Bullying tactics to ensure his way prevailed had become second nature. That said, he possessed a sharp brain and had always come top of the class in school tests.

Being leader of the pack was an automatic corollary, though not in the way his teacher would have preferred. The gunning down of a drunk who was harassing his mother had set him on the owlhoot trail at an early age. And here he was twelve years on still leading the most notorious gang of brigands in Nevada. For all his faults, there could be no denying that Juno Macklin certainly had a knack of sussing out jobs that paid well.

'We don't want to give that stagecoach any chance to swerve around them. The strong box is meant to be holding twenty big ones,' the gang boss added, drawing hard on the cigar gripped between tobacco-stained teeth. Macklin's steely grin was due to this being the largest heist yet planned by the gang of hard-nosed desperadoes. His previous crew had been caught red-handed robbing the Elko bank three years before. Only Macklin and Farlow had survived the ensuing shoot-out to live and rob another day. Such was the notoriety Macklin had garnered, there had been no shortage of eager followers wanting to join the notorious desperado.

He and his men had arrived at this remote corner of the Humboldt Sink the previous evening. They had camped out in a dried up arroyo close to the main trail, four days' ride from the nearest town of Winnemucca. Their purpose for being in such a remote locale was to waylay the weekly mail coach bound for Big Timber.

The outlaws had been up at first light, the coach being due around ten o'clock in the morning. Preparations for the surprise ambush needed time to be made effective. The desert terrain ensured that trees were few in number. This rare clump of desiccated cottonwoods providing the logs for the barricade were sustained by the rare occasions when water filled the arroyo – the result of infrequent flash floods originating in the distant mountains.

The ambush site was an isolated cluster of rocks that appeared to have been blasted from the heart of the flat wilderness. An anomaly known far and wide as Goliath's Stack, it was ideal for their purpose. All else within a day's ride was sand interspersed with scrub vegetation mainly comprising mesquite and saltbush. An occasional Joshua tree broke up the monotonous vista, its pointed leaves probing the cloudless sky.

The reminder from the boss about their share of the loot spurred the two loggers to greater efforts. A third man, ex-negro slave Moses Gate, was resting on a nearby rock having just hacked the three cottonwoods down with a hatchet. 'Come on you lazy coon, on your feet,' Whiskey Dan's gravelly vocals barked out as he dragged a sleeve across his sweat-beaded brow. 'This ain't no time to be mooning over that skirt in Reno what turned you down.'

The saloon doxie in question had snootily spurned the black man's inept advances the week before during a stop over in the booming Nevada gold camp. When his buddies had openly expressed their delight, Macklin had quickly stepped in with a blunt denunciation of the girl's lack of merit in the bedroom department. The girl was all set to challenge the brusque putdown with a stiff retort of her own when Macklin's dark scowl threatened a violent reprisal that effectively curbed her indignation. Sniffing haughtily, she kept silent and moved away to accost a more acceptable client.

This was not the first time Macklin had saved the poor guy's face. Moses had latched onto the gang boss when Macklin had saved him from a severe whipping at the hands of southern rebels who had refused to accept the days of one human owning another were over. The grateful recipient had repaid the gesture that very same day by warning his benefactor when the two disgruntled bushwhackers had tried to gun him down. That had been two years ago. Moses had since become a valued member of the Macklin Gang.

That said, the negro's former subservient life under the yoke of slavery was hard to throw off. And he still felt obliged to obey his so-called 'betters'. Accordingly, Moses levered himself up and leant his muscular physique to the weighty task. In truth he could have handled the job single-handedly. Farlow and Whiskey Dan made no further comment, acknowledging the black man's help with curt nods.

All the while Macklin was keeping a weather eye on the bunched clouds building up over the mountains of the Stillwater Range. Rumbles of thunder interspersed with flashes of forked lightning were heralding the approach of a storm. He was hoping their business of stopping the mail coach would be concluded before the threatened outburst reached them.

His other eye was focussed on the tall figure of a sentinel keeping watch from atop a rock ledge. The lofty perch offered a panoramic view of the terrain along which the expected stage coach would be travelling. The Ute half-breed had been told to raise his hand when the coach appeared then get down quick to join the forthcoming action. Charlie Wolf had abandoned his Indian name of Broken Hand and favoured a more acceptable alternative to suit his white association.

Macklin had discovered that those lurking on the fringes of frontier social order tended to be more loyal and less prone to questioning their Good Samaritan's decisions. He was always wary of hardbitten gunslingers who might get it into their heads to challenge his position as top dog. Previous attempts to usurp his leadership had been dealt with in a ruthless manner.

Nevertheless, he was still a tad unsure of his latest recruit. Rowdy Bill Hogget, an outlaw wanted for murder and bank robbery in three states, had proved his worth on their last two jobs so Macklin had no reason to doubt his reliability. But he still couldn't rid his mind of the Elko fiasco in which some critter had spilled the beans. Whether by accident or design remained a niggling mystery. Nevertheless, it had made Macklin wary of all new recruits.

Luckily the present gang worked well together. Unlike many such bands that roamed the western territories, they all rubbed along, including the fringe men. This was a vital factor that had so far enabled them to successfully evade capture. All the same, there was still something about Hogget that that didn't quite sit right. His gaze swung to where Rowdy Bill was levering a boulder to fill a gap in the barricade. It was his job to herd the passengers over to one side once the coach had been stopped.

The gang leader shrugged off the niggling itch. This was neither the time nor the place to be mulling over such issues. With the logs in position, Macklin checked his pocket watch for the umpteenth time. That coach should have been along fifteen minutes past. The lines creasing his weathered face tightened.

Had it been delayed? Or even worse, taken a different route? The teller who had been cajoled with a substantial cut of the proceeds into betraying his position at the Winnemucca Bank had insisted this was the regular monthly route. The greenbacks being carried were to pay off the numerous logging camps established around Big Timber.

That unsettling notion was fizzing around inside his head, when Wolf's raised hand gave him the signal he needed. The heist was on. Macklin heaved a sigh of relief. 'The coach will be here in ten minutes, boys.' His voice, crackling with excitement, was laced with a perceptible hint of tension. 'Check your hardware and get in position. Those turkeys are in for the surprise of their lives.'

The makeshift barricade had been erected immediately beyond a bend in the trail where it veered around the rocky promontory; too late for the driver of the stage coach to effect any retaliatory manoeuvring. Charlie rejoined the group taking up a stance to one side of the trail with Whiskey Dan stationed opposite. Mace Farlow had made the suggestion that he should hide behind the barricade where the coach would be forced to stop. 'That way we'll catch them in a crossfire if'n there's some damned fool wanting to be a hero.' Macklin had agreed, positioning himself at the far end alongside his most trusted associate.

And there they waited, each man mulling over the notion that this was the biggest job they had pulled. Farlow was dreaming about his share of the take, enough to take a nice long vacation to California. He was the oldest of the gang, being a follower rather than a leader like the younger Macklin. His musing was interrupted by the steady thud of hoofs drawing ever closer. A tight hand gripped the rosewood butt of the .36 Whitney revolver. His whole body stiffened. Only when the waiting ended and the action broke would his natural devil-may-care style take over.

Moments later, the stage coach trundled around the bend. The driver spotted the obstruction just in time to haul back on the reins, stamping his boot on the brake lever. As the coach shuddered to a halt, Macklin spurred out from behind the barricade. His gun was aimed at the guard, who immediately raised his hands.

'Keep them mitts sky bound, fella, and nobody need get hurt,' he snapped. 'Now heave that cannon over the side.' Macklin's shooter remained rock steady as the shotgun dutifully hit the dirt. A similar brusque command to the driver saw the guy likewise offering no resistance.

The rest of his men all now made their presence felt. With cocked pistols pointed his way, the driver, an old-timer nearing retirement, remained frozen to his seat. Only with the next order did he move. 'Now toss down that bag you're carrying.' Again the order was obeyed without resistance.

Macklin smiled. This was going much better than he could have hoped. 'OK, Bill, open the door and invite the passengers to step down and surrender their finery.' Only then did he notice that the window blinds were rolled down. Strange. One blind perhaps was customary, but all three including that on the door?

Suddenly without warning, all the blinds were released on both sides of the coach. At the same moment, a tarpaulin allegedly covering passenger luggage up top was cast aside. Gun barrels appeared and let fly with a furious barrage of rifle and pistol fire. No warning had been forthcoming. The driver and guard instantly threw themselves to the ground, crawling beneath the coach. From here they were both able to retrieve their weapons and add to the surprise ambush.

Whiskey Dan and Moses Gate were chopped down without any chance to get off a single round. Only then did Macklin's turgid brain cotton to the odious fact they had been double-crossed. Far from being a well-planned payroll snatch, this debacle had become a killing ground. The gang leader responded by pumping a full chamber of shots at the coach. A cry of pain told his fizzing brain that one bullet at least had struck paydirt.

'It's a set-up, boys,' he yelled. 'That darned teller has double-crossed us.' But those were to be his final words. Sat atop the paint mare, he offered an easy target. Five bullets struck his body, punching him out of the saddle. Charlie Wolf realized that resistance was hopeless. Yet still trusting in the magical potency of the lucky charm slung around his neck, he hollered out a tribal battle cry and charged the coach. The Navy Colt bucked five times, taking down a man who had raised his head too high above the luggage rack.

The reckless act of bravado was only ever going to end one way, but Wolf's demise came from a startling direction. As soon as the firing started, Rowdy Bill had quickly dropped down behind the coach and stayed there. Only with the valiant defiance of Charlie Wolf did he show himself, emptying a full chamber into the careering half-breed.

As quickly as it had blown up, the battle was over. The roar of gunfire still echoed around the killing ground where four potential robbers lay sprawled, blood seeping from their fatal wounds. Smoke from a myriad guns drifting in the static air slowly dispersed to reveal the full nature of the carnage. With all their assailants lying dead in the sand, the defenders of the payroll slowly emerged from cover.

'You did well, Hogget,' a husky voice declared from inside of the coach. A man's face appeared at the window. A gloved hand followed in which was clutched a package. The Judas took hold of the bulky envelope, making to open it. 'No need to count it. All the dough is there,' the voice continued with barely concealed disdain. 'I hope you enjoy your blood money.'

'What are we gonna do with these bodies?' Rowdy Bill thought it best to ignore the jibe as he stuffed the money into his saddle-bag.

'Let the coyotes and buzzards enjoy a surprise feast,' the chortling voice added. 'That's all they're fit for now.' Same as you, mister. Although he kept that scathing opinion to himself.

A tall broad-shouldered man in his forties opened the door and stepped down. Government agent Isaac Broffey had thick grey hair beneath his wide-brimmed Stetson. More noticeable, however, was the uniquely revered badge of a US Marshal pinned to his buckskin jacket.

Surveying the carnage, his next order was for the rest of his posse. 'OK boys, move those logs out the way and make sure our own casualties are buried proper. I'm getting too old for hard stuff like that,' he remarked, sitting on a boulder and rolling a quirly. 'But I'll say a few words when you're done.'

Once the formalities were concluded, Broffey's final comment was for the driver. 'OK Whipsaw, we're already thirty minutes behind time due to this unscheduled halt. So get them nags on the road pronto.'

Rowdy Bill Hogget had already left, heading in the opposite direction. But his disappearing profile was being followed by the searing gaze of the one man who had survived the ambush.

TWO

CHANCE ENCOUNTER

Once the mail coach was out of sight still carrying its valuable cargo, Mace Farlow emerged from cover. He was thoroughly shaken up. All his buddies had been cut down on account of the treacherous betrayal by that scumbag Hogget. His face hardened into a grim resolve to avenge his partners-in-crime.

Crawling out from where he had skulked in fear for his own life, shame now wrapped its icy fingers around his soul. Humiliation suffused his whole being at having survived without a shot being fired in retaliation while his pals lay dead. He felt like a coward. But what else could he have done?

With the heist thrown into complete disarray, Farlow convinced himself that he would have suffered the same fate unless he had taken cover.

Luckily the bed of the arroyo just to his rear had offered a gully in which to hide. Yet seeing the blood-stained corpses of his partners in crime splayed out across the battle site only served to compound the guilt eating away at his innards.

Farlow had always considered himself to be a gutsy outlaw. And he had dearly wanted to jump out letting fly with his own guns. But their attackers were well hidden with much greater fire power at their disposal. Accordingly, he figured that his only means of survival was to lie low and pray he would not be hunted down. It was a hard decision for his conscience to accept.

Nonetheless, he managed to persuade himself that a man had a duty to maintain his own survival. Playing the hero would have been the act of a brave yet foolhardy martyr. How else could he search out that double-crossing snake and repay the treachery in kind?

A sorrowful gaze rapidly coalesced into a glitter of hate as he scanned the odious slaughter. Already the desert predators were gathering. Buzzards circling overhead cawing with anticipation were matched at ground level by the morbid howl of coyotes. Farlow hustled out and dragged the bodies over to the side of the trail. There he laid them out, attempting to thwart the scavengers' gruesome intent by covering them with rocks. The laborious task took some time, but Farlow considered he owed them that much at least.

An hour later and it was time to leave. His determination to hunt down Rowdy Bill Hogget had been strengthened by the arduous chore. That was when he cottoned to the unwholesome fact that the attackers had taken all the loose horses. He hurled an impotent curse at the Heavens. Being cast afoot in this godforsaken terrain did not auger well for his continued survival. It was sheer force of habit that had seen him grab his canteen before hiding out in the arroyo, but that wouldn't last long. He was at least three day's ride on horseback from the nearest town, double that on foot.

Forced to walk out of here, his canteen would run dry long before he reached Big Timber. Thankfully water could be had in the Stillwater Mountains, although that was a stiff two-day hike across the bleak expanse of sand that encompassed the Humboldt Sink. No sense in putting it off. Stick around here and the scavengers would surely get their wish. Mace Farlow still valued his skin. Windmilling arms scared off the watching predators as he set off.

Since making a swift exit from the town of Battleaxe, Wes Longmire had abandoned the main trail. Instead, he had favoured the safer trek across country by heading due east towards the Utah border. There was sufficient food in his saddle-bag and a full canteen to keep him going for the few days needed to lose any pursuit. He slowed the golden palomino to a steady walk, his mind harking back to the unsavoury incident that had blown up in Battleaxe's biggest saloon.

The Occidental was run by a shrewd businessman

called Tuff Selman, who had employed Wes as a house floor walker. His job specifically was security, to ensure that any chancers who attempted underhanded chicanery at the numerous gaming tables were summarily dealt with. And Wes was good at his job. What he objected to was Selman introducing marked decks and loaded dice to fleece honest patrons of their hard-earned poke.

When he voiced his antipathy to the shady practice and quit the job, Selman was none too pleased. A couple of his heavies were despatched to waylay the unsuspecting gunfighter on his way back to the lodging house at the edge of town. That would have been the end of Wes Longbaugh had not two mutts decided to join the proceedings. Alerted to the presence of the dry-gulching duo by their howling, Wes had responded with split-second timing, allowing his newly acquired Colt .45 Peacemaker to speak louder and more effectively than any words.

Two men had been left dead on the main street of Battleaxe. Lingering to plead his case with the lawman in Selman's pocket did not seem like a sensible policy. So here he was drifting across the Humboldt Sink in the general direction of Delta Creek in Utah. It was fortunate that he had received a belated letter offering him the chance to earn some easy dough removing squatters from land occupied by a cattle rancher. It was a problem that had become ever more common as more and more settlers moved west.

The letter was dated two months previously; such was the precarious nature of overland communications in this far-flung corner of Nevada. The hired gunman hoped that the job was still up for grabs. His thoughts were mulling over how long it would take him to reach Delta Creek when a movement some half mile over to the left caught his attention.

The narrowed gaze homed in on a lone figure on the far side of a shallow depression. A man afoot and clearly in some distress judging by his erratic gait. Always ready to assist a fellow human being in trouble, Wes urged his mount to the gallop. When he reached the stricken traveller, the man had collapsed in a heap. Wes grabbed his canteen and leapt off the horse. He cradled the man, dribbling water between his cracked lips.

Desperate for the life-saving elixir, the man snatched the canteen in an attempt to drain the contents. 'Easy does it, fella,' Wes chided the stricken victim. 'You'll get the cramps doing that and leave us both in a fix as well.'

The man opened his mouth but was unable to thank his saviour for the timely assistance. Only his watery eyes could signal appreciation. It was another five minutes before he recovered sufficiently to express his gratitude verbally. 'Much obliged, mister,' he croaked out. 'My canteen ran dry yesterday. I'd given up all hope of reaching the Stillwaters.'

'So what are you doing out in this godawful wilderness without a horse?' Wes enquired, dribbling more water into the man's mouth. 'That's asking for trouble.'

'Had me some of that back on the Winnemucca

19

Road. I had to get away in a hurry.' He didn't elaborate, nor did Wes press the matter. He was in a similar situation, although this guy appeared to have been less successful in escaping from whatever hassle he had been involved with.

Farlow took a closer look at his benefactor, his brow furrowing in concentration. 'Don't I know you? Your face seems kinda familiar.' The grizzled features creased, puzzling over the conundrum.

'I've been around some. Job here, job there. Never staying long in any one place. You know how it is.'

A nod of understanding followed. Then it struck the older man. 'I know you as well. Wes Longbaugh, ain't it? I was in Virginia City when you took down Goldtooth Matt Stratton and his two gophers. Boy, that was some shoot-out.'

'Lady Luck was on my side that day, I guess,' Wes replied modestly, not wishing to blow his own trumpet. 'But I was mighty peaked at those duck eggs. They'd given me good reason to call them out.' A quizzical look saw him elaborating. 'Stratton shot my brother in the back when he was trying to stop them rustling his stock. The local tin star objected to my brand of administering justice so I had to skip town fast.' He coughed out a worldly-wise harrumph. 'Seems like that's become a bit of a habit of late.'

This time it was his companion who didn't pry. Instead he held out a hand. 'The name's Mace Farlow, and I'm beholden to have been saved by such an illustrious gunfighter.'

Wes accepted the friendly gesture with a familiar

nod of recognition. 'I heard tell you were riding with Juno Macklin.'

'I was until three days ago when we were ambushed while trying to hold up the Winnemucca Mail coach.' Farlow spat in the sand. The anger of resurrecting the obnoxious double-cross was starkly displayed across the aging gunslinger's twisted features. His fists clenched tight. 'Just thinking about being betrayed by one of our own makes my blood boil. If'n I ever catch up with that rat, I sure won't be calling him out for no one-to-one. That critter is too darned fast for me. Mister Rowdy Bill Hogget will get what's coming to him with a double load of buck shot. But I'll make darned sure he knows who pulled the trigger.'

'A nasty piece of work, Bill Hogget,' Wes concurred. 'Ain't never come across the guy, but his reputation for cold-blooded removal of obstacles has been passed down the line.'

'You sure ain't wrong there, pal.' Farlow struggled to his feet, keeping quiet to allow his temper to cool down before asking, 'So where you headed, Wes?'

'There's a job going across the border in Utah that could be interesting,' Wes replied. 'We can ride double to the next town where you can get a fresh mount.'

Before his companion had time to reply, Wes had drawn his revolver and triggered off two bullets. Eyes wide with shock, Farlow staggered back wondering what had precipitated the unexpected violence from his benefactor. 'What in blue blazes? he exclaimed.

Wes pointed his smoking Colt at the writhing serpent that had just slithered out from a clump of sage brush. 'Guess your hearing can't be too good, Mace. That diamondback sure had you in his sights. And he's one big fella.' Another bullet finished off the job.

Farlow's gaze followed the line of fire. The rattler was at least five feet in length, its large flat head smashed to a bloody pulp lying no more than a foot from his boot. 'Looks like I'm destined to keep being indebted to you,' he gasped out. A wan smile split the craggy facade as he dragged a grubby bandanna across a dirt-smeared face. The action was more the result of nerves than the heat. 'That was some show you put on there. Now I know for certain that draw of your'n I've heard so much about ain't no fairy tale.'

Wes shrugged off the praise, helping his sidekick mount up behind him. 'I figure we ought to reach Kingpin in two days. What you aiming to do after that?'

Farlow replied with a lackadaisical shrug. No reply was forthcoming for some time as he mulled over his options, and the conclusion reached was that they were exceedingly limited. When he finally spoke it was in a subdued, rather doleful voice.

His current predicament had laid open in no uncertain terms the true measure of his worth. A life wasted, washed down the drain. All those jobs he had pulled as a member of various factions now seemed so hollow, frivolous. Sure he had made plenty of dough, but the easy money had all been thrown away on girls, booze and high living. And here he was at the age of forty plus, old enough be the father of the young hotshot to whom he was beholden. His pockets were empty with not even the makings for a smoke. How had it all come down to this?

'You might not think it to look at me, Wes, but I used to be a brash young tearaway.' The despondent, melancholic tone full of self-reproach was not what Wes had expected. 'I practised the draw four hours a day. Figured I was a match for any hotshot foolish enough to call me out. And so it proved. But where has it got me? There's always gonna be somebody faster. And as you get older, and your faculties get slower, the time soon approaches when fear starts to take over.' The man gripped his pard's shoulder. 'You know something? If'n I could have my life over again, I'd get me a regular job, no matter how low the pay, and live a decent life.'

'I can't see you sticking at some hick job in a store or flogging your guts out on a ranch for thirty a month and found,' Wes declared, somewhat puzzled by Farlow's woebegone confession.

'Sure I would, boy. I'm living on borrowed time, just waiting on some strutting peacock to come along and finish me off.' Farlow's grip tightened on his associate's shoulder. It was as if he was trying to pass on a message. 'Ain't it the darned truth that most guys like us don't last five years? Luck's been with me so far. But it can't last.'

Farlow could see from his associate's sceptical

regard that his assertion had fallen on deaf ears. 'Most of the guys I've ridden with are now pushing up the daisies. My turn could be just around the next bend. It's too danged late for me. But a young fella like you still has the chance to follow a straight trail.'

Now it was Wes's turn to mull over his companion's soulful declaration, yet still he pooh-poohed the notion. The older man's melancholic prognostications were shrugged off. A stoically tight-lipped regard convinced himself that such gloom-laden inevitability did not apply to him. Wes Longbaugh was different. He had a nest-egg sitting in a bank in El Paso for the time he decided to hang up his guns. Maybe another couple of years following the trail of a hired gunslinger, only then would he consider settling down.

The hours passed as the palomino headed steadily east. That night while sitting round a camp fire eating Wes's meagre trail rations, Farlow sat brooding. Wes quickly picked up on his associate's melancholia. 'Some'n bugging you, Mace?' he asked when Farlow emitted a low rumble in his throat, almost like a cry of pain. 'I reckon it's always best spit out what's eating away at your craw. Bottling things up is bad for the health.'

That was when it all came bubbling to the surface. Guilt at leaving his pals to face the ambush at Goliath Stack had been grinding away at his soul. Not normally a man to express his feelings aloud, Farlow had developed a trust in this guy. A man who saves your life for no personal gain is a unique breed. Belief in the inherent goodness of another human being had been sadly lacking in the ageing owlhoot since his parents were gunned down by Quantrill's Raiders in the war.

Wes listened, not deigning to interrupt the heart-felt outpouring of self-reproach. At the end Farlow's red-rimmed gaze continued to stare into the capering tongues of flame, not wishing to meet his associate's accusing, scornful regard. Finally, Mace could stand the silence no longer. 'I guess you think I'm a yeller skunk that should be put down like a mangy cur,' he muttered glumly.

'I don't blame you one jot for saving your own hide,' Wes declared, laying a consoling hand on the other man's drooping shoulder. 'Far as I can see, it's that rat Hogget that needs eradicating, not you. Any fella in the same position would have done the same. Why toss your life away when there's no chance of turning the tide.'

'You don't hold it against me then?' A spark of hope had been rekindled in the old outlaw's slumped frame.

Wes poured them both a mug of coffee, adding a shot of whiskey from a hip flask to spice it up. 'Let's drink to you catching up with that critter and avenging your pards in time old fashion.'

Thoroughly buoyed up, Farlow's previously morose and brooding attitude lifted. Helped by the strong spirit, he regaled his associate with stories of past encounters, funny as well as hair-raising, that had constituted his life on the wrong side of the law.

In the lighter mood now encompassing the remote campsite, Wes responded with some of his own adventures.

That night, Mace Farlow was able to bed down with a smile on his face, having buried his demons in the past. The future, though unknown, would see him returning to Goliath Stack to erect a suitable tribute, but not before he had fed Rowdy Bill Hogget to the desert predators. Maybe then he would follow his own philosophy and settle down to live out his old age in peace.

THREE

BAD DAY IN KINGPIN

Next day as they approached the Stillwater Mountains, the arid terrain of the Humboldt Sink slowly gave way to a greener landscape where cattle could be seen grazing. They joined a well-used trail with a sign pointing east that read: *Kingpin – five miles.* Sighs of relief issued from the mouths of both men.

Riding double was not a mode of transport to be recommended for the long haul, especially for the guy sitting at the rear. 'My ass feels like it's been dragged through a cactus patch,' Farlow grumbled, emitting a pained lament. 'Can't wait to soak it in a hot bath. But you'll have to sub me, Wes. I ain't got two dimes to rub together.'

'Seems like it was your lucky day me happening

by,' the younger man replied. 'Good job I'm a generous kinda guy. And I suppose it'll be me paying for the grub you'll be wanting?'

'Don't worry, I'll give you an IOU for what's owed to be paid off next time we meet up.' Farlow was serious. 'And Mace Farlow always pays his debts.'

'That could be years,' Wes hawked back, imbuing the complaint with a mocking hint of scepticism. That said, he was thoroughly enjoying the light-hearted banter. 'And when you spot me coming down the trail, likelihood is you'll hide behind the nearest rock 'til I've passed.'

'You've gotten me all wrong, buddy. I'm a trustworthy guy. Ask Juno Macklin when you see him.' The ageing gunman's face suddenly darkened as realization of what he had just said hit home. That situation would never be happening. The sneering features of the treacherous skunk responsible swam before his eyes. 'And you, Rowdy Bill Hogget, will be top of the payback list.'

The hissed declaration effectively terminated the genial exchange. For a brief spell, taut silence enveloped the riders, but it was only temporary. By the time they were approaching the town of Kingpin, the morose cloud had dispersed. During the short period they had known each other, the two unlikely travellers had become firm buddies.

It felt to both men as if they had known each other far longer than the few days it had taken to reach the isolated settlement. Farlow felt a certain paternal responsibility for this younger version of himself, while Wes respected the older gunman's wise counsel, even if he had no intentions of following it.

Stuck on the edge of the Humboldt Sink, Kingpin was more a collection of shacks thrown together beside the shallow crossing point of the Muddy Mary Creek. All this latest pair of visitors were concerned about was acquiring a fresh horse for Farlow and some much-needed vittles before they parted company.

The only place likely to supply their needs was the Laughing Coyote saloon. A grinning depiction of the said scavenger painted bright red and sporting a large black Stetson was nailed to the front of the wooden edifice. Wes guided the horse over to the hitching pole.

The two men went inside, pausing to scoop aside the smoke-laden atmosphere. It was a rough and ready establishment with little in the way of comforts. Drinking and gambling appeared to be the sole distractions on offer. 'What, no dancing girls?' Farlow laughingly grumbled at the lone bartender, who continued to study a one-page news sheet without looking up.

'Whiskey, beer or cards,' came back the laconic grunt. 'Take your pick.'

'Sure is a tough choice,' Wes said, ruefully scratching his head. 'What d'yuh reckon, Mace, beer or whiskey?'

For once in his life, Mace Farlow's priority was elsewhere. 'Any place around here to wash up?' he asked, rubbing his sore behind. 'We've both collected enough dust and sand to start a new desert.'

The lethargic sluggard cast a languid arm towards a door at the rear. 'There's a pump out back. Two bits for a cold wash.' His mood lightened somewhat as if he was doing them a favour, adding, 'and that includes soap and towel.'

'What about a hot bath?' Wes enquired, without much hope of a positive response. And he was right.

'Jolly John the barber has a couple of tubs,' the laugh-a-minute beer-puller espoused. Wes perked up, only to have his hopes dashed straight away. 'But he's closed for the weekend.'

'Guess it'll have to be a cold one then.'

'Good job it's hot as Hell out there,' remarked Farlow.

Wes nodded, tossing the coins on the bar top. The two weary travellers sauntered across to a door at the rear, Wes tossing his hat onto a table in readiness for a drink and some grub to go with it. A notice advertised beef stew and dumplings, which would go down a treat after a week of trail fodder.

While they were scraping the dirt from their sweaty bodies out back, a noisy commotion broke out on the far side of a wooden fence on the street out front. 'Looks like the Saturday hootenanny has started early,' Farlow commented. 'That should bring a smile to the miserable old goat who runs this place if nothing else does.'

Hair slicked back and feeling a whole lot lighter after ditching the trail dust, the two men ambled back into the saloon. Straight away, Wes sensed that trouble was in the air. A tight frown laid the dark

shadow across his tanned face as he scraped up his
hat from where it had been thrown on the floor. Four
jabbering cowpokes had commandeered their table,
and they already looked and sounded as if this was
not their first stopping off point.

Abe Kelty was the culprit, and he had clearly given
the brash action little heed. 'Get them drinks over
here, pronto,' the loud-mouthed Nevadan cowpoke
called across to the slouching barman. 'We've gotten
us a thirst that needs quenching, ain't we boys?'

Turkey Jack, who ran the Red Rooster at weekends,
hurried across carrying a tray with four glasses and a
bottle of red label whiskey. It didn't do to keep the
Kelty boys waiting. Nor did he take the risk of serving
them with the rot gut reserved for wandering drifters
like those two who had just taken a wash out back.

Abe, together with his two brothers, Seb and Chet,
and a cousin known merely as Moon, ran a small
cattle outfit at the far end of the Gerlach Valley. They
had registered it with the Nevada Cattle Breeders'
Association under the brand of the K Bar 4. More
than likely it was Kelty cattle that had been spotted by
Farlow and Longbaugh on their approach to
Kingpin.

Although Abe was the youngest of the clan, the
others acknowledged him as their leader, more due
to his bullyboy manner than any skill at cow punching. Abe's quick temper was legendary in the valley,
as was his expertise with a handgun. Only the previous week the hot-headed tearaway had shot and
wounded a travelling drummer for allegedly selling

him watered down whiskey.

The four men had settled themselves at the table, with Chet dealing out the cards for a game of poker, when a shadow fell across the table. It was clear to Wes from the space separating these fellas from the other drinkers that they oozed trouble, especially when they had been at the hard stuff.

Nobody wanted to earn their displeasure, but many of those watching closely could see that the tough-looking jasper now approaching the table had evil intent in his forbidding gaze. The man stopped beside the table, yet still the Keltys were unheeding of his proximity. Strange seeing as the babble of conversation had faded to a throbbing murmur.

A low voice, casual yet imbuing an ill-omened hint of menace, was thus all the more able to make its presence felt. 'This table is already taken.'

Only then did the four men deign to look up. It was Abe who replied with a sneering retort that saw his buddies chortling. 'You're right there, mister. By us. Now go take a hike.'

Farlow, who was standing to one side, instantly sensed the likely outcome of this confrontation, the direction the wind was blowing. His hand rested on the butt of the .36 Whitney. Never one to back away from trouble not of his making, the tough old brigand stepped forward, grabbing the whiskey bottle off the card table. The unexpected interference caught the cowpokes off guard.

Evincing a casual aplomb, he poured himself a glass, which was downed in a single swallow. 'Good whiskey,' he said, smacking his lips in appreciation before pouring a second one. 'But a bad answer to my pard's question'

Not used to their blustering tactics being challenged, the cowboys were momentarily stunned into silence. Mouths hung open in startled amazement. Only when the contents of the glass were tossed into Abe's face did the bubble burst. Spluttering inanely having been taken by surprise, brother Seb was the first to react. The eldest Kelty leapt to his feet, clawing at the gun on his hip. 'Why you dirty lowdown saddle tramp,' he hollered out.

The revolver was only half drawn when the poor sap was punched back by the force of a .45 chunk of hot lead. It had originated from the gun of Wes Longbaugh. Blood gushed from Seb Kelty's chest. That was the moment all hell broke loose in the saloon as the other patrons dived for cover on the dirt floor. Farlow took hold of the whiskey bottle and flung it at the mirror behind the bar, further adding to the chaos.

'Time we was out of here, buddy,' he called, adding his own gunslinging prowess to the melee by lifting the hat from Moon's head.

'Guess you're right there,' Wes replied as the two men quickly yet methodically backed towards the front door of the saloon. Both were hard-boiled gunfighters not prone to panicky decisions. 'And I didn't even get to have that drink.'

Once out on the street, Wes jumped on his horse, Mace commandeering one of those parked by the

Keltys. Shots were aimed at the saloon door to temporarily deter any pursuit, giving them a fighting chance of escaping unhindered. Spurs then dug deep as they galloped away in a cloud of dust. Their sole aim now was to put some distance between themselves and the pursuit that would surely follow.

With Seb dead, the rest of the Kelty clan would be out for revenge, and spilling the blood of the perpetrators would be a number one priority. With them knowing the local terrain, it was vital that the fugitives somehow lose them. Three miles beyond the town limits, the trail could be seen entering the confines of a broad expanse of dense pine forest. 'If'n we can reach that, there's a good chance of throwing them off'n the scent,' Longbaugh shouted above the steady pounding of the galloping horses.

His buddy nodded. 'We can leave the trail at any point and head up into the mountains,' he added, slapping the mustang on the rump. 'Ain't no way they'll cotton to which direction we've taken.'

Ten minutes later the two fugitives entered the gloomy confines of the close-packed forest. Little in the way of vegetation existed at ground level due to a lack of daylight being able to penetrate the thick canopy. Progress slowed as the narrowing trail twisted and turned along the valley bottom. Great care had to be taken to avoid low branches that reached out, seeking to drag them to the ground. Wes couldn't help but consider where such a trail would lead. Only when they encountered a patch of bare rock was it possible to abandon it.

They followed a course up through a narrow gully, allowing the horses to pick their own way among the loose stones. Emerging into daylight above the tree line some three hundred feet above, an upper side valley opened out ahead. It gave the impression of hanging above that which they had recently abandoned.

Thereafter they were able to follow a broad shelf of bare rock deep into the heart of the mountains. On their right a weaker layer of the rock had been worn down by a thundering torrent of churning water that had carved out a deep trench. On the far side, more stands of pine could be seen marching up a precipitous slope until the rock face barred any further advance. The air was much fresher up here, where bunches of grey cloud blocked out the heat of the sun.

But it was the head of the valley that drew their attention. A mighty waterfall over five hundred feet high could be seen plunging over a broad lip. It gave the appearance of a silver snake striking ever downwards to bury its fangs in the rock pool below. The mesmeric sight was awe-inspiring, but more interesting to the fugitives was the small cabin occupying a grass-covered ledge below the towering ramparts of rock. It had been sited some twenty feet above the eddying maelstrom of the plunge pool out of which the river continued down valley channelled through the rocky trench.

The two men paused, each trying to determine whether or not the cabin was occupied. 'No horses in the corral,' Farlow observed. 'Looks abandoned to me.'

Wes was inclined to agree but urged caution before they investigated further. 'Could be you're right, Mace. Just the same, reckon we should move on down slow just to make sure.' He turned around in the saddle. 'Looks like we've managed to lose any shadows. So this would be a good place to stay overnight.'

Ten minutes later, with no movement detected, the two men drew rein outside the cabin. From this position, the grumbling roar of the cataract could be heard, but was out of sight on the far side of a jutting promontory. They tied up their horses in the corral and, with guns drawn, made a slow approach to the closed door of the one-roomed shack. To these men, caution was second nature.

For Mace Farlow especially, it was just one good reason why he had survived for this long in such a precarious profession. He opened the door and stood back so as not to present a clear target for any incumbent. All remained silent as the grave, apart from the ever-present thunder of the waterfall. They stepped inside, adjusting their gaze to the dim interior.

It was bare with little in the way of comforts. 'Looks like this could have been a gold prospector's shack,' Farlow said, picking up a gravel sifting pan.

The observation was confirmed when Wes pointed to a small set of weighing scales perched on a home-made cabinet. 'Maybe the claim didn't pay well enough to stick around,' Wes speculated, sitting down on one of the rickety chairs. 'But it'll sure do for us overnight. And there are even two cots to sleep on. Luxury indeed for two jaspers in need of rest and relaxation.'

Mace laughed as he searched around for signs of any grub that had also been abandoned. A downcast look at his pard told its own tale. 'Not so much as a pinto bean or even a stick of jerky in the place.' Mace rubbed his grumbling stomach. 'And I'm starving.'

'Well you struck lucky when we met up,' Wes replied, opening his saddle-bag. 'I got me a loaf of bread and a jar of blueberry jam. Chow fit for a king.'

The older gunman's eyes lit up. 'Boy, I ain't eaten blueberries in a coon's age.' Farlow's eyes popped as Wes hooked out the large bowie knife strapped to his belt and proceeded to saw off a couple of thick slices. With a generous dollop of the gleaming blue delicacy swathing the bread, Farlow accepted the food with reverence, tears in his eyes. 'You sure are being mighty considerate to an old ne'er-do-well like me, Wes. And I ain't gotten a thing to offer in return.'

'I ain't asking for nothing,' Wes said, shrugging off the guy's obviously sincere appreciation as he settled down with his own simple repast. 'Except maybe to hear some more of those fairytales of daring-do from the vivid imagination of a genuine old-time gunslinger.'

The tongue-in-cheek remark saw his buddy balking at the very notion. 'Hey you young whippersnapper! Those stories weren't no figment of my imagination.' He paused, eyeing up his partner, before noting the sly smirk while munching on the wholesome fare. A slug of whiskey from his buddy's hip flask along with a cigar were equally welcomed before he added on a more serious note.

'Sure I could tell you about a heap more scrapes I've somehow managed to survive.' Farlow blew out a plume of smoke as he considered his options, of which there were many. But he had another more pressing piece of advice to impart. 'What I reckon would be more useful is to remind you of that advice I handed out while we were crossing the Sink. Gunslinging is a mug's game, boy.' An accusatory thumb jabbed at his own chest. 'Look at me. Ain't I proof of that? Find yourself a decent gal and settle down. Take a mundane job and live to be a hundred.'

Wes could see from the older man's earnest expression that he was truly concerned for his pard's welfare, yet still he remained unconvinced. Like all young studs on the prod, he felt invincible. So on this occasion he merely nodded and listened with only half an ear. His mind was over the border in Delta Creek and that new job.

By the time they had finished the meal and drunk the last of the coffee, the clouds had dispersed, allowing the sun to set over the western rim of the canyon. They wandered outside to make sure the horses were OK before ambling round the rocky excrescence. The fading sunlight was glinting on the tumbling water spout, transforming it into a mesmeric flaming arrow fired from the bow of some cosmic archer. Both men stood on the lip of the deep plunge pool, their gaze imbibing the wonder at that glorious sight.

It was Wes who broke the spell. 'Reckon we should hit the sack if'n we're planning to quit this territory in the morning,' he proposed, tossing the butt of a dead quirly into the swirling waters below. 'Nevada's getting a bit too hot for me.'

'You ain't the only one, pal,' Farlow concurred, giving his associate a tentative look that hinted of more to come. 'Mind if'n I tag along for a spell. There's nothing left round here for me except more grief.'

'What about that promise you made to find Hogget?' Wes enquired.

A shrug of resignation followed. 'Reckon he can wait a mite longer. Fact is, the skunk could be any place by now. I'll catch up with him soon enough. In the meantime, you and me seem to be mussing along quite well. So what do you say?'

Wes hesitated. He was not used to having a partner. 'No offence, Mace, but I usually work better alone.' He quickly qualified the putdown on seeing the disappointment clouding his new buddy's visage. 'We can ride together as far as Delta Creek. Maybe I can persuade the guy running the Pine Cone ranch over there that two guys are better than one. After that we'll see what happens.'

Mace perked up. 'Much obliged to you, Wes. I'm certain that us two could work well together.' Wes hid his doubts regarding such a partnership under the corollary of a yawn and stretch to indicate sleep was called for.

FOUR

TRAPPED

The three remaining Kelty boys had been forced to give up the chase when their quarry's trail ran cold. Abe threw a curse of frustration at the surrounding ranks of pine trees. Any chance of continuing the pursuit now was being blotted out by the lengthening shadows of approaching dusk, yet still he hated giving up. It was left for the prudent counsel of his elder brother, Chet, to persuade him that continuing the chase was futile and dangerous.

The hunt had initially been delayed by the theft of Moon's horse, a fresh mount having to be borrowed from the livery stable; a futile grumble that Abe now resurrected. 'That weren't my fault,' Moon grumbled. 'He could have taken anybody's.'

Abe wasn't listening. 'You murdering skunks won't get away that easy,' he railed at the dark ranks of pine forest, zealously vowing to resume the search at first light. With some reluctance he realized that continuing would indeed be useless. Cussing at the wind, he swung around and led the way back to Kingpin.

Back in town, Moon was all for continuing their abandoned Saturday night bacchanalia. Abe rejected that notion outright. 'We need to be up early with all our wits alive.' A piercing look of animosity conveyed the threat of dire consequences should his order be ignored.

They persuaded the liveryman to give them an empty stall in the barn to spend the night. The normal charge of two bits per man was passed over by the prudent ostler in view of the circumstances, not to mention Abe Kelty's scowling regard. His dead brother was given a resting place of his own until such time as the body could be returned to the ranch for burial alongside their deceased parents.

It was still dark when Abe kicked the others into wakefulness. With the false dawn lightening the eastern backdrop, the three men along with their dead kin strapped to the saddle of his horse set off on their rancorous quest. By the time the burning orb had crawled above the serrated rim of the mountains, the grim-faced line of riders had reached the place where their quarry had quit the main valley trail.

In their haste to escape the previous day, Wes and his buddy had ignored the golden rule. Always mask your trail when danger threatens. It wasn't much, but the ever-vigilant Abe Kelty spotted the lone hoof print etched in a pat of soft earth where the fugitives had left the main trail. 'Lookee there, boys,' the defiant cowpoke snapped, jabbing a finger at the tell-tale evidence. 'This must be where they turned off hoping to fool us.'

Chet hawked out a snort of agreement. 'Perty soon you're gonna have the revenge you deserve, brother Seb,' he snarled patting the slicker-swathed corpse on the rump. 'Then you can rest in peace alongside Ma and Pa.' The others nodded in sympathetic accord.

With a revitalized passion for settling the score, the three riders turned up the same gully their prey had taken the day before. More positive indications in the form of broken twigs and hoof prints lent encouragement that they were on the right track. They pushed on eager to finish the grim task of retribution.

At the rear leading the dead man's horse, Moon was secretly living up to his name with regular slurps from a bottle of his power-packed homebrew. Abe's attention was concentrated on following the trail. Had he realized his cousin was becoming increasingly soused, sparks would have flown along with the bottle. He knew that the three Keltys would need to be sharp as tacks to effect a successful outcome of their hunt.

The new sun painted the eastern rim of the mountains a brilliant orange as they entered the deep hanging valley known as the Devil's Cauldron. With Abe leading the trio, he was first to spot the two horses tethered in the corral of the old cabin. His eyes glittered with anticipation. 'We're in luck, fellas,' he averred with gusto. 'Now you see why we had to set off early. Them two murdering skunks ain't surfaced from old Panhandle's place yet, so we can easy get the drop on them.'

The three men dismounted, ground-hitching their horses, then carefully approached the cabin. 'Keep your heads down, boys. Those varmints could emerge any time soon.' Abe's terse remark saw him drawing the .36 double-action Cooper and checking the load. Not being a cartridge pistol, he always carried three spare chambers, fully loaded. Seb favoured a .44 Remington. Both of them also carried a Henry carbine apiece. Moon was no *pistolero*, preferring to rely on his trusty old Spencer carbine.

Slowly they moved nearer the cabin, taking advantage of the rocky nature of the landscape for cover. 'You fellas wait on my word before hauling off,' Abe ordered. 'We need them both outside in the open. Then it's hallelujah and goodbye!'

They would not have long to wait. All the while Moon had been taking crafty snorts from the bottle, now almost empty. As a result he had positioned himself away from his cousins, being fully aware of Abe's reaction on discovering the truth.

Meanwhile, inside the cabin and totally unaware of the danger hovering outside, Farlow announced that he was going down to the creek for some water. He had unearthed half a sack of coffee hidden in a cupboard. 'It's old stuff, but beggars can't be choosers,' he grunted, his snout crinkling as he sniffed at the grounds.

His pard merely scratched his head, stretching the stiffness from his limbs, 'Anything is better than nothing. I'll get a fire started in the grate. We need to be heading off soon. I don't reckon those cow-pokes will just sit back and let the grass grow under their boots.'

Farlow commandeered a bucket, not forgetting to strap on his gun rig. It was an automatic reaction – old habits never died. 'See you in ten minutes, Wes,' he cheerfully threw back over his shoulder. 'Have we enough bread and jam left to see us on our way?'

'Guess we can stretch it, and a roll-up each for good luck.' The door opened and the unsuspecting outlaw stepped outside.

He was immediately spotted by Abe, who laid a cautionary hand on his brother's arm. 'Wait for the other jasper to emerge, then give 'em hell,' he whis-pered.

But across the open sward, Moon's inebriated brain had forgotten the stipulation. 'Yahoooo! Here they come, boys,' he shouted, jumping to his feet. Without thinking, he triggered off a round from the Spencer. Had he not been half cut, the shot would doubtless have removed Mace Farlow from the affray, but Moon's swaying frame had kyboshed that notion. The bullet went wide, allowing Farlow to react in the only way he knew how.

The holstered revolver leapt into his right hand, situations akin to this were no rarity in the deadly game he played. Three shots were loosed off in the blink of an eye and one struck the lumbering bush-whacker in the leg. Moon went down, rolling in agony on the ground. 'I'm hit, boys,' he howled, rolling in the dust. 'Help me out. I can't move.'

'It's only a flesh wound, you drunken sot,' Abe growled back. 'Now drag that useless carcass of your'n over behind that rock and get to shooting like what you're meant to.' The strident cursing from Abe Kelty at his cousin's brainless reaction was drowned out by the response from his and Chet's own guns. This was no time for futile castigation. That would come later. Now it was lever, aim and fire; lever, aim and fire as both Henrys roared. The silence of moments before was shattered by the harsh crackle of rifle fire.

Still triggering off at the unseen assailants, Farlow backed towards the open door of the cabin, but age had caught up with him and he was not quick enough. A bullet struck him in the chest. Wes pumped a half chamber of shells at the puffs of rifle smoke, vital seconds allowing him to jump out and drag his pal back inside. And just in the nick of time. The door was slammed shut as more bullets hammered into the plank barrier.

Farlow's face creased up in pain. The wound was pumping blood. An old piece of rag was stuffed against the damaging chest injury. 'Keep that wad tight, Mace,' Wes hollered. Panic was threatening to override his natural cool demeanour under fire. 'I'll give these critters something to think on.' His gun began to answer back, the instinctive calculation of the born gunslinger springing to the fore.

The response from the two surviving assailants now supported by Moon's Spencer was clear and precise. Another kin shot down had strengthened their resolve for blood. The battle continued with each side trading shots. Pretty soon it was clear that the attackers had come prepared with plenty of ammo to back their play.

During a lull in the attack, Moon, now completely sobered up, was moaning about his leg wound. 'What am I gonna do, boys?' he whined from the far side of the clearing. 'This leg is giving me jip and I can't stop the bleeding. You gotta help me.'

Abe honked out a growl of annoyance. 'Quit you're griping. You'll live. Just tie it off with a tourniquet.' Even though he felt like strangling his addle-headed cousin, Moon was still blood kin. And that could not be passed over even if'n he was a drunken toe rag.

Inside the cabin, Wes was berating himself for leaving his rifle in its scabbard. So certain was he that the hunters had been duped, he had foolishly allowed his guard to drop. And now they were both paying the price. After checking Farlow's wound a second time, it was obvious he needed a doctor fast if'n he was to survive. That was clearly not going to happen. Nonetheless, he did what all pals do under similar circumstances and attempted to play it down.

'It don't look too bad, Mace,' he insisted, while trying to staunch the gory dribble oozing from his pal's chest. 'Soon as its dark, we'll sneak away and get you to a sawbones.' But his assertion held little in the way of confidence. To all intents and purposes, sundown felt like a lifetime away. And their ammunition was running low. With only the reserve cartridges in their shell belts, the Keltys with rifles as well as handguns, held the whip hand.

But the forced smile did not fool the injured man. 'I ain't gonna get out of here,' Farlow grunted, sucking in air. 'No need to soft soap me, Wes. I know the score. One day soon it was bound to happen.'

'Don't talk hogwash,' Wes rebuked his sidekick, struggling to hide the anguish behind the optimistic facade. 'There's plenty life in you yet.'

But Farlow brushed off the phony confidence. 'We both know the truth. I been in enough scrapes involving bullet wounds to know this time it's for keeps. Ain't no way I'm coming out of this pickle.'

He gripped the other man's arm in a surprisingly firm hold. 'But it ain't too late for you. Promise me when you get out of here, you'll change your ways and put up your guns. Live a proper life. Or you'll end up like me, choking your guts out in some grubby shack.' His grip strengthened. A fervent gleam of hope urged his younger counterpart to do the right thing. 'Promise me!'

For a moment Wes hesitated before acceding to the heartfelt plea. He knew there could be no more displays of false optimism. 'OK, Mace. I promise.'

The dying man smiled, then removed a gold watch and chain from his vest pocket. 'This was my pa's. A keepsake, the only thing of any value I got left. It was gonna pay for a decent funeral. You take it. Perhaps it will remind you of that pledge when the devil starts whispering in your ear.'

For the first time in his life, Wes Longbaugh, the tough gunslinger, shed a tear. The lone droplet etched its sinuous path down through a stubble-coated cheek, falling onto the hand gripping his arm. 'But I don't see how I'm gonna escape from here with only six shells left.' The downcast rumination was not for his own safety. He was more than prepared to go down fighting alongside this man he barely knew yet regarded like the father he had never known.

Farlow's grip on life was fading rapidly. Rheumy eyes glassed over, his laboured breathing heralding the end. Somehow he managed to rally for one last entreaty. 'I gotten that covered, boy. . . .' He paused, wheezing as the death rattle gripped his throat. 'You can make it outa here . . . by doing as I tell you. Now listen up.' There was another longer pause while he struggled to draw air into his weakening lungs. 'It's a stunt . . . I pulled once before . . . when Saratoga Johnny and his gang were chasing me across the Animas plateau near Durango.'

Wes was forced to bend low to hear the barely audible croak as his dying pard briefly related the escape plan. 'You got that, Wes? Do as . . . I say and you'll win through this crazy caper. Now help me up.'

Wes knew what his buddy was setting up, but his instinctive reaction was to refuse. 'I can't just let you throw your life away for me,' he contested.

49

'It's the only way, boy. Let's not kid ourselves. We both know I'm finished anyway,' Farlow insisted. 'You still got your whole life ahead. This way I won't have to die in vain.' The flickering gaze was just able to perk up one more time. 'Every time you open that watch, it'll reminder you where a wasted life on the wrong side of the tracks will lead.'

Wes looked away, not wishing to display the alien emotion threatening to overwhelm his self-control. Gathering himself for the final countdown, he reluctantly heaved his pal onto his feet and helped him over to the door.

'Give me a last slug from that whiskey flask, then I'm outa here.' They both shook hands. 'And you remember that pledge, Wes. I'm holding you to it. My ghost will be watching to make sure you don't yield to temptation.' The distraught gunslinger could only nod as he gingerly opened the cabin door.

Farlow palmed his revolver. 'Good luck, buddy,' he croaked out, turning to obey the grim reaper's summons. 'See you in the hereafter.' Then he lurched out into the open, triggering off the last of his ammo.

Almost immediately there was a furious reply from the hidden attackers. Farlow's futile response was cut short as he went down in a hail of lead. All Wes could do was grit his teeth and watch his pal dance around like a demented marionette as the bullets punctured his body. Angry frustration now boiled over. He cussed and yelled at the top of his voice, emptying the last of his bullets at the hidden foe.

The throaty wail of torment gave the attackers the false impression that their concentrated fire power had reaped its reward. 'Hear that, boys,' Chet hollered out, making to leave the cover of the rocks. 'We got the bastard.' Not so ready to acclaim victory, Abe pulled his brother back down. 'Not so fast,' he cautioned. 'Give it five minutes. We ain't in no hurry. He could be trying to fool us. We'll approach the cabin carefully from different directions when I give the word. He can't cover both sides at once.'

Wes took advantage of the unexpected lull in hostilities to slip out the back door. Quiet as a mouse, he hustled across to where the rocky shelf terminated on the edge of the waterfall plunge pool. And there he proceeded to implement the subterfuge outlined by the now deceased Mace Farlow.

Heart in mouth, he peered over the rim at the thrashing ferment below. There had to be a place to hide beneath the overhang for him to fool those varmints into thinking he had met a watery end. Without that he was stumped. The consequences didn't bear thinking on. Scrambling along the edge, he prayed avidly for his deliverance. And then he spotted it – a tree close to the lip whose roots had forced a way through the cracks in the rock.

A more thorough inspection was enough to know the twisted root system would hold his weight, but time was not on his side. Already he could hear the bombastic calls for surrender coming from the far side of the cabin. The moment of no return had arrived. Removing his hat, he flicked it like a gyrating plate towards the churning maelstrom below. Down, down it floated on the displaced current of air, whirling like a child's spinning top before finally settling in the middle of the pool; a tiny island dipping and wallowing amidst the foaming effervescence.

Wes lowered himself gingerly onto the outermost branch, testing its sturdiness. It trembled under the unaccustomed burden, creaking and groaning. Nervous strain caused his chest to tighten as the intruder prayed the branch would hold firm. And so it did. Confidence restored, he slid further under the overhang up against the bedrock.

And only just in time as well. Above the two uninjured Keltys had arrived. Moon had been left to lick his wounds out front. Would they be fooled into thinking the obvious? Or would his makeshift refuge be sussed out? Wes held his breath, not daring to move a muscle.

'Looks like the critter tried to escape by swimming across the pool,' Chet remarked pointing down at the hat.

'He'd never have gotten across there so fast,' scoffed Abe. 'The water's too darned rough. We'd have spotted him easy.'

'Guess he must have panicked then; or hit his head on a rock,' Chet added, staring at the wavering piece of evidence. 'Whatever happened, he didn't make it. The whirlpool has done the job for us.' He looked towards the cluster of white bolls drifting by overhead. 'At least you've gotten your revenge, Seb.'

No more than six feet from where Abe and Chet

Kelty were discussing the ruse into which they had
fallen, Wes Longbaugh was struggling to remain
calm and still. The confined hideaway had given him
cramp in his left leg. All he could do was stretch the
offending limb and hope these jaspers would fall for
the stunt, then move off. Eyes tight shut, he clung on
for dear life.

After what seemed like a month of Fridays, the
unsuspecting hunters finally appeared to be content
that the chase was over. Abe cast a smug look towards
the floating headgear. He pumped off a couple of
rounds from the Henry, which punctured the brim
and caused it to tip over and disappear beneath the
churning water. The sudden blast of gunfire almost
caused Wes to lose his precarious hold.

'Reckon we should head back to Kingpin now and
get that useless lump seen to by the sawbones,' Abe
concluded, shouldering his carbine. Their simple-
minded cousin might not be the sharpest knife in the
drawer, but he made an important contribution by
producing the best home-brewed hooch in the
county. It was liquor that provided the Kelty boys with
a much-welcomed second income.

The exchange of words by the two brothers faded,
allowing Wes to relax somewhat. He still remained
where he was, clinging to the tree root beneath the
overhang. And there he stayed until sure they had
departed the scene of conflict. When he finally
emerged from hiding, his first task, gruesome but
essential, was to secure a spade and bury his old
buddy.

Seeing the bullet-riddled body lying outside the old shack like a heap of discarded rags brought a lump to his throat. They had not known each other long, but the older guy had made a distinct and lasting impression. With careful reverence, he lifted the body and laid it down beneath the shade of the cottonwoods. And then he began to dig. The tough chore of breaking up the unyielding ground helped control the anguish of losing a valued friend in such a brutal manner.

Finally done, Wes bowed his head, a woebegone expression clouding craggy features. Some suitable words over the makeshift grave concluded with a reaffirmation of his pledge to quit the life of a hired gunfighter. But then the abject look stiffened into one of gritty resolution. 'But you'll have to bear with me for a spell, pard, while I put it on the backburner,' he quietly yet tenaciously pronounced. 'Justice has to come first.'

The stony glint in his eye boded ill for the killers.

FIVE

AND THAT'S A PROMISE!

His own hat having been instrumental in saving his life, Wes commandeered that of his dead pal. The high crown was pummelled into a shape favoured by the new owner. Then he mounted up. Now that he knew the direction in which they were headed, he could easily catch up with the Kelty brood of vipers. Then it would be payback time. In full.

Wes was mightily relieved to see that his horse had been left in the corral along with that of his interred buddy. Far more significant, however, was the rosewood stock of the Winchester poking out of its boot. In their elation at mistakenly figuring they'd achieved their terminal goal, the Keltys had ridden off unheeding. With no shells left in his revolver, this was a vital acquisition if Wes was to turn the tables on those murdering scumbags.

Now it was he who was playing the hunter. *Quid pro quo* – tit for tat – an eye for an eye. Roles had been reversed. And he intended to take full advantage of the position he had managed to secure. A doleful gaze scanned across to the lonely grave. He removed his hat in respect, the one bequeathed by Mace. 'Once this is over,' he muttered under his breath, extracting the pocket watch and holding it reverently, 'I truly promise to hang up my guns.' And he meant every word.

Tracking the unsuspecting quarry proved to be a simple matter of merely retracing the outward journey, but he would need to run them to ground well before they reached Kingpin. With surprise on his side, he made good time. The winding descent back down into the main valley found him increasingly on the alert.

It was around midday that he spotted smoke rising above a cluster of trees up ahead. This could only be the Keltys, who had stopped to rest their mounts and cook up some grub. Perhaps they were celebrating the success of their vengeful mission. A low yet menacing growl gurgled in Wes's throat. These turkeys were in for the shock of their lives. Here was a golden opportunity to catch them unawares.

The palomino was secured to a tree as Wes crept warily through the dense undergrowth. Each step closer to his objective was tested with care to ensure no sound betrayed his presence. The Winchester was pointing forward when suddenly a voice to his rear barked out a warning. 'Hold it right there, mister.'

Chet Kelty had gone down to a nearby creek to fill their canteens. On his return to the camp hidden among the trees he had spotted the lurking figure moving through the brush. And judging by his crouched posture, this was no wandering drifter hoping to share a meal and some idle gossip. A closer inspection saw the cowpoke's eyes widen with shock.

His mouth gaped wide on recognizing the guy supposedly drowned in that plunge pool in the Devil's Cauldron. Chet shook his head to ensure he was not dreaming. It was him alright. The critter must have somehow fooled them. And here he was sneaking up on the camp, figuring to get the drop on them. A twisted grin split the leathery contours of a face intent on reprisal. 'You heard me, fella. Raise those hands. Any fancy tricks and you get a hunk of lead up your ass.'

Wes was equally startled by this sudden reversal of fortunes. He froze, silently cursing his luck. The guy had caught him red-handed, but he knew that surrender was a certain one-way trip to perdition. 'OK, you got the drop on me,' was the despondent reply. 'I surrender.' The Winchester fell to the ground.

'A wise decision,' the cowboy intoned with a sigh of relief. 'Now turn around slow and easy so's I can get a good look at the man who killed my brother.' Figuring he now had this skunk at his mercy, Chet's body relaxed. 'Abe is gonna be mighty surprised when he sees what I've found.'

Shoulders slumped as if to register his capitulation, Wes made to obey. As he did so, unseen by Kelty, his right handed reached across his own body, gripping the bone handle of the sheathed knife. Quick as a flash, he whipped out the deadly blade and hurled it at the unsuspecting cowboy.

Chet was given no time to react, the razored edge burying itself in his chest. Stuck between his ribs, it had punctured the heart. No amount of frantic tugging could remove it. The gun fell from nerveless fingers; wobbling legs gave way as life rapidly faded. His mouth flapped open desperately trying to utter a warning, but no sound emerged as he tumbled in a heap.

Now it was Wes's turn to heave a sigh of relief. Lady Lucky had changed her affections. A reflex action of the fingers could so easily have triggered off a random shot from Chet and given away his presence. It took some effort with a boot stuck on the dead man's chest to heave the gore-smeared blade free. Wiped clean, it was then slotted back into the sheath. One down, two to go.

Before leaving the killing ground, Wes appropriated Chet's handgun and spare ammo – an 1863 New Model .44 Remington converted for cartridge use. The new owner nodded his approval. 'Not as good as the latest Colt revolvers, but it'll do for now,' he muttered to himself. Stealth and caginess were now called for to remove the two remaining dry-gulchers from the picture.

Within two minutes his acute hearing picked up

the murmur of conversation. It was coming from the far side of a rocky upthrust. Great care was needed as he scrambled up the back slope. Height overlooking the camp on the far side would give him the upper hand. Once atop the shelf, he crawled towards the edge and peered warily over. And there they were. Abe Kelty was strutting around while forking a plate of beans down his gullet. 'Where in thunder is that lazy critter?' he ranted at the man lying beside the fire chewing on a stick of beef of jerky. 'It can't take all this time just to get some water from the creek.'

Moon wasn't listening. A hand pawed at the blood-soaked rag covering his bullet wound. He winced in pain. 'I need a doc, Abe,' he bleated. 'The bullet is still in here and it's hurting bad.'

'One more word from you and I'll finish the job,' his fractious brother snapped back. 'It's your own fault for jumping out like that. This is what supping too much of that rotgut does for you. '

Wes had heard enough. He poked the Winchester over the edge of the rock shelf and called out a stentorian mandate. 'This is the end of the line, Kelty. Undo your gunbelt then step away.' Abe swung round, fear-riddled eyes searching for the hidden adversary. 'And don't be figuring that the other varmint will come to your rescue. He's buzzard bait now.'

That was the moment Wes showed himself. Like his brother, Abe Kelty was stunned into silence seeing his nemesis standing there, elevated on high like some ghoulish spectre risen from the dead. 'Bu . . . but you're supposed to be. . . .'

All Wes's attention was focused on the one cowboy he considered most dangerous. Moon's injury was clearly visible, as was the pain he was suffering. 'As you can see, mister, this ain't no daydream. Now shuck your hardware.'

But ignoring Moon was a mistake. A simple cowpoke he might be, but he was just as ruthless as his other kin when the chips were down and blunt action was called for. And when sober he was also a crack shot with the Spencer now lying by his side. Unfortunately for him, this was not one of those occasions. His injury and the extra snorts consumed to help ease the pain had slowed him up. The blundering movement to raise the rifle was spotted by Wes, who responded immediately by cutting loose with the Winchester. Moon had made his second and final error of judgement. This time he would not be requiring the services of a doctor, merely a grave digger.

The sudden explosion of gunfire dragged Abe back to the reality of his situation. Somehow this guy had survived the clutching embrace of the whirlpool. Three of his kin down, he would go the same way if'n he didn't act now. A hand grasped hold of his own hogleg. The gun rose and triggered a couple of shots at the exposed figure up on the shelf. Even though Wes was out of effective handgun range, the hostile resistance threw him off balance. He ducked down out of sight, giving Abe the chance to dash across to where his horse was tethered.

He leapt into the saddle and leathered the animal

into motion. Wes was not fazed. With calm deliberation he slotted the Winchester's stock into his shoulder and took careful aim along the upper barrel. In normal circumstances he would have balked at shooting a man in the back. This situation was anything but normal. The thought of Mace Farlow's bullet-riddled torso with more holes than a politician's promise made him see red. He shook off the anger and concentrated.

Crack, bang!! The double report echoed across the clearing as two .44-40 shells winged their way towards the fleeing target in quick succession. Abe Kelty didn't stand a chance. Wes stood up and mouthed a silent comment that sped across the ether. 'If'n you're up there watching, pal, the pledge starts as from now. No more hankering to promote a gun-toting reputation for Wes Longbaugh.'

But words come easy to the tongue when there is nothing to hinder their avowed intention. Anyone can make a promise. Keeping to it can be a much more difficult task. Especially for a man with the reputation acquired by Wes Longbaugh.

And so it was to prove when he wandered into the town of Delta Creek. Since leaving the site of his last confrontation, allegedly his last, Wes had ridden hard for the border. A week later he crossed into Utah by way of Tomahawk Pass. Hopefully he could now put the past out to graze and begin a new life, as he had pledged to Mace Farlow. Still heading in a general easterly direction, he skirted the southern edge of the Great Salt Lake Desert to reach the town from which the job of squatter removal had originated.

The nearer he came to Delta Creek, the more he was mulling over whether such a job could be accomplished successfully without resorting to gun play. Some squatters went peaceably while others fought back. Was it worth the risk? The death of Mace Farlow and the outpouring of his forlorn life story, originally disregarded, now shook the hired gunfighter to the core. The ride east had given Wes ample opportunity to mull over the warnings espoused by his dead associate. He could now clearly see where such a life would end up.

But shucking a reputation willingly sought after and achieved was proving hard to cast aside. Mere mention of his name often saw respectable folks cringing away, not wishing to be tainted by a sinister aura that enveloped all those who followed the profession of a hired gunslinger. On two occasions over the last week he had stopped at ranches and asked for work, only to be turned away unceremoniously when his name was mentioned. Had the die been cast long ago?

As Wes Longbaugh, was he destined to end his days coughing out his guts on some dusty street, shot down by a younger version of himself? He could always change his name, just disappear, but that was the coward's way out. The very notion of slinking around waiting for the next snarled challenge heralding recognition by some gun-hungry kid did not sit well on proud shoulders.

And so, with much to think on, he drew rein outside the Ponderosa saloon in Delta Creek. Uncertainty as to the way forward was a vexatious issue that he could not ignore. Dismounting, he tied up the palomino and slapped the dust from his weary frame. As usual, he entered the dim interior of the saloon slowly, eyes panning across the array of drinkers and gamblers.

A sixth sense would tell him if trouble was brewing, but nobody paid him any heed so he sauntered across to the bar and ordered a beer. The cold beverage would help focus his thoughts. He sure needed something to keep his pledge alive, and his self-respect intact.

Perhaps if he visited the Pine Cone ranch he could gain an impression of how things stood, always assuming the job was still up for grabs. There was only one way to find out. He called across to the bartender. 'Could you direct me to a guy called Ivor Meek who runs the Pine Cone ranch?'

Mouth open ready to deliver the required information, the barman was cut short by a brusque retort from the other end of the bar. 'Who wants to know?' The gruff demand immediately silenced the mutter of conversation as all eyes turned towards the speaker.

He was a tough-looking jasper, whose very presence caused the other drinkers at the bar to shrink away, sensing a showdown was on the horizon. The sneering regard was a challenge in itself, intensified by a stance that left no room for doubt. This jigger's intervention was no friendly gesture. A talon-like right hand hovered above a low-slung shell belt that screamed out – *Beware! Gunslinger on the prod.* The two men held each other's gaze, neither prepared to back down.

Wes knew he should have tried to defuse the tense atmosphere that had suddenly blown up. Backing away, hands raised to show he did not want any trouble, would have been the sensible option. But personal self-esteem once again nudged aside the pledge he had made in good faith at the time. It was proving to be far harder an achievement than he had ever considered.

He levered his rangy frame off the bar and faced the hard-boiled tyrant. 'The name's Wes Longbaugh. . . .' He paused to allow the declaration to sink in. A gasp went up from the watching crowd, whose automatic response was to slink back further. 'and I'm here, if'n it's any business of your'n, to see the boss man about a job he's offered.' He pulled out the letter and waved in front of the challenger.

The man's left eyebrow, akin to a black worm crawling across a dirty stone, lifted slightly. It was the only intimation that the infamous handle had struck a note. He gave the blunt-edged introduction a meaningful sneer intended to convey his disdain. 'Well Crazy Rafe Hubbard has beaten you to the punch, mister. Better sling your hook and make tracks. The job's been taken.'

Wes was not to be sidetracked. 'That so,' he replied, taking a slow drink of beer. 'Maybe I'll check that out with the organ grinder and not the monkey.' He set the glass down and straightened up, a sure fire signal that he was not about to back down. The deliberate insult had been uttered before he realized what the upshot would be.

Hubbard's boorish features twisted up into the crazed snarl that had secured his nickname. Globules of slaver dribbled from betwixt gritted teeth. 'Why you no good piece of crap,' he rasped flexing his gun hand. 'Nobody speaks to Rafe Hubbard like that and gets to walk away.'

The growled epithet would have cowed most adversaries, but Wes Longbaugh merely returned the demented gawp with blasé indifference. 'I just did, monkey. Now you just walk away or get carried out in a wooden overcoat.'

The casual delivery only served to wind the hard-case up all the more. A guttural roar rumbled deep in Hubbard's throat as he grabbed for his shooter. The revolver had barely left its holster when two bullets slammed into the gunman's chest. Blood poured from the open maw in a ghoulishly red fountain. The crazy coot had met his match with a terminal result from which there was no reprieve. He staggered back, grabbing for the bar. But his legs gave way, dead eyes glassing over.

White smoke drifted from the pointing Remington revolver held by the perpetrator. Nobody had seen the lightning draw, such was the speed of its accomplishment. Displaying the cool manner of someone for whom this was no new experience, Wes casually blew the smoke from the barrel. He twirled the gun on his middle finger and with arrogantly expert dexterity slotted it home before turning back to the bar to finish his drink. 'Now then, barman,' he enquired as if nothing untoward had just occurred. 'You were about to tell me how to reach the Pine Cone spread.'

Yet again the awestruck barman never got to make a reply.

SIX

NO ROOM AT THE INN

'Just keep those hands on the bar top, mister.'

The firm authoritarian voice was punched out with vigour, the aim for instant obedience being assumed. Sheriff Tuborg Griffin had been passing the Ponderosa when the fracas inside drew his attention. One look through the grimy window was enough for the wary tin star to know that trouble with a capital T was about to be unleashed. The name given by the tall stranger was well known to him, and sufficient inducement to make him hesitate before intervening.

Wes Longbaugh! What in thunderation was he doing in this part of the country? Griffin knew him by reputation only, a ruthless hired gunslinger who had somehow managed to remain on the right side of the law even though he had at least ten notches on his gun butt. And the guy had unfortunately landed in Delta Creek with the inevitable response.

Gunslingers of his ilk drew unwelcome attention like bees to a jam pot, and there will always be some foolish jackass ready and willing to prove his manhood. Two of them in the same town sent a cold shiver down Griffin's spine. The ageing starpacker had been more than a mite concerned when Crazy Rafe Hubbard had arrived the week before to work for that land grabber Ivor Meek.

Both of these guys boasted predatory reputations only the hardiest or most reckless protagonist would challenge head on. Tub Griffin was not one of those, at least not any more. Sure he had cleaned up a few wild cow towns in his younger days. And bringing in Fiery Jack Spade single-handedly following a spate of robberies in Hayes City had been the pinnacle of his career. But those days had long since fallen by the wayside. All he wanted now was to see his time out in peace.

Tub had initially thought Delta Creek would be one of those places; he should have known better. The town council had not hired a once-renowned town tamer just to help old ladies across the street. After scratching beneath the surface layer of apparent serenity, he had discovered that Delta Creek was no different. In keeping with many such towns scattered across the western frontier, such serenity was a mere pipe dream, like pissing into the wind. By then it was too late, the die had been cast and Griffin had taken the job. And to Tub Griffin, the proud wearing of the revered tin star demanded duty and responsibility.

Accordingly, the tough lawman, once known as Double Tap for obvious reasons, now hung back. He would intervene in this fracas at a time of his choosing when safe to do so. The climax arrived, as with most of these showdowns, in a blur of action that shattered the apparent calm before the storm.

And as expected, Crazy Rafe was the loser in this particular battle. That was the moment Tub Griffin made his presence felt. At least one more gunslinger had earned his place on Boot Hill, now he had to face a man for whom he held the highest respect on account of a grim reputation that had once again been proven beyond doubt.

Well past his best he may have been, but the ageing law dog was not short on pluck. When Wes made to turn around, Tub halted the move with forthright assurance. 'Stay right where you are, Longbaugh. One false move'll be your last.'

A momentary silence followed as time stood still before Wes spoke up. 'Glad to see you're still sharp as ever, Double Tap,' he responded with a blithe hint of flippancy, yet making sure to keep his hands flat on the counter. 'I'd remember that sour mash voice anywhere.'

Griffin was visibly perplexed, taken aback. His heavily ribbed brow puckered, although it did not hinder his vigilance regarding the danger this man posed. The gun remained steady as a rock. 'I've heard tell of you by reputation only, fella. How come you know me?'

'It was in Abilene back in '67 when the first cattle drives came up the Chisholm Trail from Texas. I was a greenhorn cowpoke with Ned Solomon's Rocking Chair outfit. Boy, was that some rip snorting town for a cocky young sprout fresh off the trail and eager for some fun.' Wes hawked out a nostalgic guffaw, at the same time slowly turning around to face this legend from way back.

Griffin allowed the tentative manoeuvre as his own thoughts harked back to those earlier days. His gaze held no sign of recognition. And why should it? As a marshal keeping order among the myriad comings and goings in a wide open cow town, he had been kept too busy to remember one young hotshot cowboy.

Not so for Wes Longbaugh, however. His own regard held a deal of respect. Same old drooping moustache graced the upper lip shaded by thick eyebrows like a pair of coon tails. A bit fuller round the middle perhaps, and grey was now the dominant hair colour. That said, the firebrand marshal of Abilene had changed little in the intervening years. 'I recall you taking down Wild Billy King cool as you please with that famous double tap.'

Griffin eyeballed the renowned gunslinger with studied curiosity. He nodded slowly as recall of that notorious clash was resurrected, but the momentary wisp of replay was soon discarded. He was not to be overawed by ingratiating flattery; that dish was best served cold, and raised a sniff of disdain. Too many slick gun hands had tried throwing him off guard in too many washed out towns. And he was still here while most of those gunnies were pushing up the daisies.

'Seems to me like that particular recollection didn't teach you anything, Wes.' The jaundiced response was laced with cynicism. 'Only five minutes in town and already there's blood been spilled. Trouble follows varmints of your ilk round like a bad smell.'

'This weren't of my seeking, sheriff,' Wes countered openhandedly. 'He gave me no choice. Ask anybody here. The skunk drew first.' Nods of accord confirmed the killer's claim of self-defence.

The lawman accepted the petition but was in no way about to lend his support for the outcome. 'You ain't gotten my drift, mister. So I'll repeat it. Hired gun toters bring trouble. I want you gone from here pronto. Finish your drink then hit the trail. There's enough tension in Millard County between ranchers and squatters without you adding to it. You've got one hour.'

Griffin deliberately holstered his revolver and turned his back to leave the saloon. 'One hour,' he repeated over his shoulder. 'Fail to meet the deadline and you'll have a personal demonstration of that Double Tap handle. And I never miss.' It was a piece of bluff theatre developed over the years where reliance on trickery and sheer bravado were fundamental to catch his opponents off guard. Truth be told, Tub Griffin was not that fast on the draw, and a polished gun hand like Wes Longbaugh could easily take him down. At these moments he prayed that a brash approach would pay dividends.

And so it proved. Exactly on the hour, the doughty sheriff of Millard County was tipping his hat to the infamous hired gunman as he trotted past the jailhouse. Wes returned the gesture, wondering how he was ever going to rid himself of a reputation that would enable him to hang up his guns as pledged to Mace Farlow. So far, that promise had fallen on stony ground through no fault of his own.

After the legendary lawman had left the Ponderosa, Wes had shrugged off the distraction of a dead man lying at his feet to repeat his original question. 'You gonna tell me how to find this guy Ivor Meek then?'

The rotund beer puller had given him the directions along which he was now headed. The Pine Cone ranch lay five miles to the south-east. He soon arrived at a break in the trail where a prominent sign board pointed the way beneath a wooden gateway boasting a pair of long horns. A barbed wire fence stretched away into the distance marking off Pine Cone land. With Crazy Rafe Hubbard out of the picture, the job of troubleshooter was once again vacant.

But what caught Wes's attention was the notice in blue paint that read: *Private Land – Squatters will be shot on sight.* A red cross had been daubed roughly across the sign and the wire beside the entrance had been cut. The skin around the gunman's eyes tightened. This was not going to be the simple job he had expected. These nesters were resisting. More gun play was inevitable.

He pulled out the pocket watch and flicked it open. Inside, the stiffly posed image of a young man peered back at him. Mace Farlow would have been around his own age when he visited the photographer's emporium. 'So what should I do, Mace?' he muttered to himself. 'A guy has to earn a living somehow.' But he already knew the answer his old associate would have delivered to that question. And the use of guns did not figure in the response.

Accordingly, Wes Longbaugh tore up the job offer into little pieces and scattered them in the dust. He nudged the palomino forward, heading towards the distant Henry Mountains. Once he quit Millard County, perhaps he could find some quiet town and settle down just like he had pledged to do.

SEVEN

GOOD ADVICE

Wes kept on riding ever eastwards until he felt
certain he was clear of Utah. Negotiating the
complex maze of canyon lands characteristic of
eastern Utah had taxed all of his tracking skills. As a
result he was confident that nobody holding a
grudge against his recent depredations could have
followed. Yet only after he had been given confirma-
tion by a passing farmer that he was now in Colorado
did he feel able to relax. Three weeks had passed
since he had quit Delta Creek.

The contrast in the landscape was strikingly
evident. Rolling grassland hemmed in to the east by
the Uncompahgre Plateau was fed by the San Miguel
River, the source of which was the mighty bulwark of
the Rocky Mountains. Dark green ranks of ponderosa pine and aspen contrasted markedly with the

richly verdant tint in the valley. Carpets of golden columbine and blue gentian intermingled with the bright red of poppies.

Wes smiled to himself as he surveyed the lush terrain. This was good cattle country. Perhaps now he would have the opportunity to make good on that pledge. Get himself a regular job. And not before time.

The first settlement he encountered bore the name of Saw Tooth. Masses of logs piled high on the outskirts of the town were a clear indication of a major activity carried on here. He paused to survey what lay before him. As with all fresh human encounters, the instinctive need for caution took over. An initial inspection revealed a bustling township with folks going about their everyday business.

But how would it prove once he had delved below the surface? A leading question that only a visit to the local saloon would provide. Wes's casual progress along the main street was being watched by two young boys. Frank and Tommy Hardacre were always curious about newcomers to Saw Tooth. Accordingly, they followed the progress of this lone stranger who sat on his horse in the manner of the tough hombres they both eagerly devoured in the dime picture papers that were becoming ever more popular with younger readers.

'He looks just like Dead Eye Charlie Bucket in last week's story,' Tommy Hardacre remarked. He was the elder brother by two years and always liked to impress his younger kin with knowledge gleaned from the garish picture stories. When Wes dismounted and tied up outside the Sidewinder saloon, Tommy was quick to note the low-slung holster and gun rig tied down for a fast draw. 'See there, didn't I tell you,' Tommy gabbled excitedly. 'He's a gunslinger if'n ever I saw one.'

Young Frank stared open mouthed, accepting his brother's evident assumption. 'I'm gonna be the fastest draw in the west when I grow up,' Frank declared deftly, wielding the wooden pistol his father had carved for him.

'You'll never be as fast as me,' Tommy snorted scornfully, drawing the old .36 Navy Colt his uncle had given him, minus the firing pin, of course, for safety.

'Will so!' came the blustered retort. 'Let's follow him and see what happens. He might be here for a shoot-out.'

That notion had not occurred to Tommy Hardacre. 'You think so?'

The two boys watched as the newcomer entered the saloon. Once inside, Wes paused as usual to survey the interior. Being the middle of the day, it was empty save for a lone drinker propping up the bar. The newcomer leaned against a display cabinet, reaching into his pocket for the makings. That was the moment a distinctive rattle found him jumping away from the cabinet. The tobacco pouch fell to the floor.

The drinker and barman chuckled uproariously. 'Didn't the name of this place make you think twice, mister?' the drinker hawked out. 'This is the Sidewinder saloon. Hank here keeps half a dozen of the critters, just in case trouble breaks out. The threat to release them snappers soon restores order.'

'And over on the other side is another pal of mine,' the barman added gesturing towards the glass case. Wes gingerly peered over at the full-grown Gila monster. 'I had him shipped in from Flagstaff only last week. Best not to stroke him though. Them jaws. . . .'

'You don't need to tell me, fella,' Wes replied, gathering up his fallen goods. 'I've met these varmints before. Not exactly the greeting I expected. Bad for the heart.' He tapped his chest. 'All I came in for was a drink.'

'Give the man a beer, Hank, and put it on my tab,' the drinker asserted with a smile as he wandered across, hand outstretched. 'I reckon we've had our fun. Don't want a stranger getting the wrong impression of our town. Welcome to Saw Tooth. Tate Lincoln's the name. I try to keep order around here.' The lawman waited expectantly for the other man to respond accordingly.

That was the moment the sunlight glinted off the five-pointed star pinned to the man's chest. Wes hesitated to accept the invitation. Shaking hands with the law would be a new experience, one he was wary to accept. It was a bit like handling one of those rattlers. Old habits die hard.

Although an outright antagonism towards those who administered the law had never quite raised its ugly head, previous dealings had always been of a suspicious, distrustful nature for both factions. The negative manner in which he had been forced to leave Delta Creek immediately sprang to mind.

Keenly astute when it came to sizing up a newcomer, the lawman instantly sensed an antipathy towards his profession. The smile slipped from his face. Yet still he held out a hand. A man was always regarded as an equal if not a friend until proven otherwise. 'Do I sense an aversion to those who wear the badge?' he volunteered in a low yet firm voice.

'The law and me have always had a . . . shall we say cautious understanding. Maybe you won't be so eager to expend a welcoming hand when you know it might get stung . . .' He paused, fixing a gimlet eye onto the stoical starpacker before dropping his bolt from the blue. 'by Wes Longbaugh.'

Both marshal and bartender stiffened, visibly stunned by the revelation. But Lincoln quickly recovered his composure. 'Is there anybody likely to turn up in Saw Tooth looking for you?' he enquired in a flat tone. 'I don't want more trouble than I already have around here.'

'If'n I knew that I could earn my living as a mind reader.' Nonetheless, Wes accepted the proffered hand. It was a weird, off-the-wall experience. 'That sure is a first for me, marshal. Shaking hands with a lawman. Feels mighty strange. Now you know the score, I reckon you'll be eager to scan those wanted dodgers clogging up your desk.'

'Am I likely to find one for Wes Longbaugh?'

'Why don't we go find out?' Wes turned to leave the saloon. 'Then we'll see whether I'm still gonna be invited to have that drink. Best keep it on ice, Hank.'

'You're a cool one and no mistake, Longbaugh,' the lawman averred, following this notorious gunslinger onto the street.

'In my game it's the only way to stay alive,' came back the stark rejoinder. They stepped down off the boardwalk and were about to cross the street to the law office when a distinct sound assailed Wes's acute hearing. His reflexes were instantaneous. Twisting and palming the Colt .45 all in one sinuous movement, the hammer snapped back ready to discharge its lethal charge. Chet Kelty's Remington had been exchanged for a Peacemaker at a gun merchant's.

Just in time, he held back. There standing behind him was Tommy Hardacre clutching the cocked Navy that was shaking like a leaf. The kid's face was white as a sheet, terror gripping his innards. 'D-don't sh-shoot, mister,' he stammered out. 'I was only playing with Frank here. W-we didn't mean no harm.' He held the gun out. 'See the firing pin's been removed.' His younger brother was no less frozen to the spot, the wooden pistol now lying in the dust.

The man's face did not relax. The grim look remained fixed and immutable. Finally, after what seemed like a lifetime to the poor kid as he stared down the barrel of a real gun, Wes Longbaugh slowly released the hammer and slotted the gun back home. Then, in a measured response heavy with forewarning, he gave a brief yet penetrating piece of advice.

'Don't ever again walk up behind a man pointing a gun, boy. As you just found out, it's the way to an early grave. You were lucky to have met Wes Longbaugh and not some reckless desperado who shoots first without thinking.' He paused, keeping the kid pinned down with that menacing hard-eyed stare when the open jaws of both Hardacre boys hit the floor. This was serious business. 'There's nothing wrong with playing at being a tough gunslinger if'n that's all it is. But too often I've seen it get out of hand when a boy gets to thinking he's a man. Get my drift, fellas?'

The boys were totally mesmerized. Was this really the famous gunfighter they had heard so much about? And here in Saw Tooth talking to them? 'Are you really Wes Longbaugh?' young Frank blurted out. The shock of almost being shot down appeared to have vanished. His face shone with hero worship.

'You two not heard a thing I've being saying?' Wes rasped out, snapping his fingers in their faces to break the spell. 'You nearly stepped over the edge just now. So in future, use those guns for shooting varmints or deer hunting. Two-legged critters tend to fire back. What job does your father do?'

It was Tommy who replied in a somewhat embarrassed voice. 'He runs the furniture store with Ma.'

'It was Pa that made this pistol for me,' young Frank blurted out.

'And a noble profession it is too, vital to all our lives,' Wes emphasized, leaning closer while examining the carved object. 'Where in tarnation would we be without fellas who can make stuff like that? Now run along. And just remember – it's not the gun that does the killing, but the man who pulls the trigger.'

'OK, you guys,' Sheriff Lincoln said in support, clapping his hands. 'You heard the man. Your pa's over there on the stoop and I reckon he needs some help.'

'S-sure thing, Marshal. See you around, Mister Longbaugh, sir,' a thoroughly chastened Tommy Hardacre espoused. Coming face to face with the grim reaper is apt to stifle the most romanticizing brain, even that of a young boy. He was now fully aware that play-acting with guns must not be allowed to encroach into the real world, where life and death are no figments of the imagination.

'That was good how you dealt with young Tommy,' Lincoln declared. 'I'm impressed. Most gun slicks would have cuffed him round the ear if'n they hadn't already dropped him.'

'He needs to learn the truth of where gun play can lead,' Wes mused half to himself, thinking on his own path through life. 'It only takes one mistake to launch an innocent kid down the trail to perdition. And I should know.'

The lawman lit up his pipe and puffed it into life as they crossed the street to check on those dodgers. He was still unsure of this man and whether his sudden appearance in town was going to be a magnet for trouble he had no wish to attract.

Inside the office, perusal of the latest batch of wanted posters soon made it clear that Wes

Longbaugh had somehow managed to steer clear of official wrong-doing. Being a hired gunfighter and bounty hunter was a fine line to walk. On numerous occasions he had brushed the edge, always managing to scrape through untarnished. Sooner or later, though, he knew that line would be crossed. It was only a matter of time if'n he continued along the same trail.

'I have never been a man who judges others on rumour and gossip,' Lincoln declared after putting the pile of dodgers back in the desk drawer. 'I take a man as I find him. And so far you ain't given me cause to figure you're here to cause me any grief. I need a new deputy to help me keep the peace around here.'

'My impression is that it seems a quiet town. What do you need help for?'

'There's a powerful rancher by the name of Leroy Devine,' the marshal explained, indicating for Wes to take a seat. He removed a bottle from a cupboard and poured them both a drink. 'He's after taking over all the land in the valley. The guy's started by fencing off the main water supply that abuts his current land holding. Most of the land round here has no legal holding so it's up for grabs. . . .'

Wes sighed. He'd heard it all before, and been involved in the result he knew was about to be explained. So he quickly interjected. 'Don't tell me. The smaller outfits are none too pleased and have threatened to take action.'

Lincoln nodded. 'They've already started. Only

small stuff at the moment. Threats of retaliation and a bit of rustling. Devine's Star LD brand is easy to change. We've had the Southern Cross and even the Box Elder appearing on auction days. Neither side is ready to back down. That's why I need help. Somebody who'll stick around with the guts to use that gun he's toting wisely. I reckon you're that man.'

'So who's in the right in all this hoo-hah?'

'Neither side as far as I'm concerned,' Lincoln sighed, puffing on the dead pipe. 'And I'm stuck in the middle trying to keep them apart.'

This was not the kind of talk Wes wanted to hear. He stood up ready to depart. 'That's a dangerous place to be, marshal. I'm not the guy you want. I came here looking for a peaceful life. Seems to me like getting involved in a range war would be like jumping from the frying pan into the fire. I made a pledge to shelve my guns and get a regular job. Thanks for the offer but no thanks.'

Lincoln was not convinced, nor was he ready to give up. 'Easier said than done, Wes.' He topped up their glasses. 'There's two kinds of employer round here. Those that would pay top money for your services like Devine, and those who could only afford peanuts in comparison, like the logging operators. And even they'd shy away knowing your reputation. But this a growing town, which means I can pay good wages to the right man.'

He paused, carefully studying the gunfighter's reaction. These guys worked for money, yet still there was no positive sign that his offer was being seriously considered. Wes still had his hand on the door handle ready to leave, so Lincoln decided to adopt a different tack.

'Come in with me as an official deputy and you'd be using those guns to keep the peace, not break it.' The lawman removed a worn badge from his desk and pushed it across. 'You'd be doing me a mighty big favour.' The obdurate stony look had mellowed somewhat, so Lincoln put forward his most appealing draw. 'Why not come over to my house this evening for dinner. My daughter is an excellent cook and we can talk some more over a glass of finest Scotch whisky. No charge and you can walk away with no hard feelings if'n you're still set on fulfilling that pledge.'

'Guess there can't be any harm in that,' Wes replied. Food and mention of a daughter were the cheese in the trap.

Tate Lincoln allowed himself a congratulatory smile. Get a tough hardcase like Wes Longbaugh on his side and his job would become a lot easier. 'I'll walk you over to the National Hotel and book you in. The job also comes with board and lodging.'

Once in his room and alone, Wes lay down on the bed. He needed some quiet time to reflect on his options. Soon he had fallen asleep, but it was not to be a dreamless relaxed interlude. Subliminal visions of his past life, dark and hostile, flashed across his mind, broken by the frequent report of gunfire. He awoke some time later bathed in sweat, unsure where he was. His breath came in short panting gasps.

Staggering to his feet, he splashed water over his face from the wash bowl, eager to expiate the nightmarish effects of the hallucination.

Now he was fully convinced that Mace Farlow had been right. But would pinning on a lawman's badge be the answer to his dilemma? That was a burning question yet to be answered.

EIGHT

STRANGER THAN FICTION

When Wes arrived at the Lincoln household, the door was opened by an exquisite vision in blue. Flowing locks of blonde hair encased a face of celestial delicacy that immediately took the visitor's breath away. Kay Lincoln's clear-eyed magnetism, however, failed to mar the somewhat frosty regard with which she greeted their dinner guest. Hat in hand, Wes stumbled over the doorstep.

'Good evening, Mister Longbaugh,' the girl said, taking his hat. 'We are honoured to have such a . . .' She deliberately hesitated before adding, 'distinguished guest.' Her obvious cynicism was not lost on the visitor. Holding the mesmerized gunslinger's gaze, she flung the hat behind her. It spun threw the air to make a perfect landing on a hook attached to the opposite wall.

Wes was more than a tad impressed. Beauty coupled with skilful adroitness made for a potent blend. He was about to give voice to a crass remark aimed at regaining the upper hand when common-sense came to his rescue. All he could manage was a trite, 'Do all your guests receive such a unique welcome, Miss Lincoln?'

The lawman's arrival on the scene saved him any further embarrassment. 'I see that Kay has been displaying her party piece,' Lincoln declared, giving his daughter an admonitory look. 'She always reserves it for those unlucky folks who have yet to meet her exacting standards. Happens all the time. Just ignore her.'

That was a caveat Wes found impossible to follow as Tate Lincoln led him through to the dining room. All the while his eyes were fastened onto the swishing skirt disappearing into the kitchen. Tate soon brought him down to earth with a glass of wine and a fine cigar.

Conversation over the excellent meal was led by the marshal, who filled Wes in on the details of what was happening in Saw Tooth and its environs. The town had grown up as a logging settlement but had since diversified into cattle ranching dominated by Leroy Devine's Star LD outfit. Only in the last year had settlers primarily interested in growing crops begun arriving.

Lincoln was warming to his subject. 'That was when the trouble started. Cattle and sodbusting have never been good bedfellows. And Devine figures that being the first rancher to bring cattle into the valley gives him a free rein to ride roughshod over recent incomers. I can sympathize with his gripe. But it's the way he's dealt with it that gets me worried.'

Only half of Wes's attention was on the lawman's explanation. His eyes struggled to pull themselves away from the swaying hips moving back and forth across his vision. The lawman couldn't help but notice the direction in his guest's mind was veering. 'You understand what I'm saying, Wes?' he pressed.

'Sure I do, Tate,' Wes replied, dragging his thoughts back to the real reason for his invitation. By the time dessert was served they had gravitated to first-name terms. 'So has this Devine jasper broken the law?'

Lincoln hesitated. 'Not exactly. But he's intimidated smaller spreads into selling out at knockdown prices by hiring in gunslingers to back his play. And rustlers have been summarily dealt with by vigilante courts convened at his ranch. I want the official courts to decide on such issues, including who has right of occupation on land once deemed open range. But out here we're stuck on a limb far from the nearest big city. It's a difficult tightrope to walk on your ownsome.'

Kay Lincoln chose that moment to get in on the conversation. Thus far she had merely offered desultory comments of a mundane nature. She now felt the time was right to voice her simmering suspicion regarding their guest's motives for turning up in Saw

Tooth. Over the meal, it had become patently obvious that she harboured a grudge against him.

'What Pa hasn't told you is that the previous deputy was lured away into working for Devine,' she interjected during a brief lull in the conversation. 'Bill Hogget was all nice as pie at first, promising to back Pa up while attempting to ingratiate himself with me.'

Wes Longbaugh's face turned an ashen grey. Mention of the notorious outlaw was like the kick from a loco mule, a body blow that struck deep.

Little thought had been given to Hogget since the violent passing of Mace Farlow. Yet here was the guy who had been instrumental in causing that untimely death back in that hidden Nevada canyon. And being able to pull the wool over the eyes of a guy like Tate Lincoln made him extra dangerous. He would need all his skill and dexterity to outwit such a protagonist.

Wes couldn't help concluding that the hand of fate had drawn him to Saw Tooth. At that moment it sure seemed that way. Persuaded by the girl's frosty reception and his pledge to Farlow, Wes had virtually decided that Saw Tooth held no future for him. He had been about to voice his refusal of the offer when this startling upset had been delivered.

What would Mace be urging him to do now? The old outlaw had been determined to avenge the death of his comrades-in-crime at the hands of that treacherous rat. He could almost hear the snarled tones of his old pal urging him to do the right thing. Here was his chance to close the door, set the record straight, wipe the slate clean once and for all.

He knew what had to be done. There could be no walking away now. His responsibility was clear as the driven snow.

As she stood there, hands on hips, berating the previous incumbent of the post, Wes couldn't help conceding that at least the fella had good taste in women. Kay was not slow to heed their guest's similar motives. Her dazzling gaze hardened. 'And my betting is that you're cut from a similar cloth. Make no mistake, once Devine knows you've pinned on a star, he'll come offering you a similar deal.' Her shoulders stiffened as she turned away, deliberately flaunting her contempt.

Wes was about to deny the accusation when Tate Lincoln intervened. 'So is Kay right? Will you sell your soul for a mess of potage as the Good Book declares, or are you made from sterner stuff?' He lit up his pipe, studying the other's man's response to the double challenge from both father and daughter.

'Hand over that badge, Marshal.' He murmured almost as an afterthought, his eyes lifting slightly to acknowledge his dead pal's urging. 'And just to set the record straight, ma'am. Wes Longbaugh doesn't welsh on a deal.'

The marshal's breath hissed out in obvious relief. 'I'd almost given you up as a lost cause,' he declared, hustling across the room to pin on the revered badge of authority. 'What changed your mind?'

'Must be something in the water round here,' Wes replied nonchalantly, staring at the shiny hunk of metal. 'Either that or I'm losing my marbles. Wearing this sure feels mighty peculiar.'

'You'll soon get used to it, and it'll strengthen my hand dealing with a loose cannon like Leroy Devine.' Lincoln held out a hand, which Wes accepted. 'Get some sleep. I'll show you around tomorrow and give you the rundown on what other duties a lawman has to fulfil apart from the obvious.'

Wes turned his attention back to the taciturn Miss Lincoln, whose cool regard appeared to indicate a less eager response to the appointment. 'And what have you gotten to say, ma'am?' He held up a cautionary hand. 'And before you answer, I can tell you straight that I ain't no Rowdy Bill Hogget. Me and him are most definitely riding different trails.'

A shrewd judge of character, Kay Lincoln's detachment was well placed. She now speared him with a caustic glower. 'I see you and Hogget have already locked horns, Mister Longbaugh. Could that perhaps be the reason you have decided to take the job? My verdict is that revenge for some past grievance has driven any desire to help the community into second place?' An accusatory regard challenged the gunslinger to deny her assertion.

Wes was taken aback by the unexpectedness of the incisive allegation. He paused to gather his thoughts. 'You might well have something there, ma'am,' he admitted, rather diffidently conceding the girl's clever judgement of his motive. 'Although it's not me that wants revenge. I'm just the means of wiping the slate clean for a good friend.'

The lawman's previous zeal had faded somewhat. 'Is this true, Wes?'

Caught out good and proper, Wes turned his attention back to the somewhat puzzled Tate Lincoln. 'Don't worry, marshal, I'll play my part in keeping the peace. But I'd go through those dodgers a bit more carefully in future. Likely you'll find one with Hogget's ugly mug on it.' He couldn't help adding with a wry smirk, 'not to mention a generous reward for bringing him to justice.'

Over the next few days, Wes soon settled into his new role. Initially it had been an uncomfortable experience far removed from his normal manner of operating. The Hardacre boys had followed him around for a spell, goggle-eyed that the famous gunslinger had become a lawman. However, the dull routine of checking stores and collecting rents had soon palled. This was not what they expected from a man with Wes Longbaugh's reputation.

The man in question did have a few run-ins with drunks plus clearing up disputes between neighbours, none of which had involved the infamous Leroy Devine. That gentleman appeared to be keeping a low profile. On his third day in the job, he and Tate Lincoln were studying the latest batch of wanted posters when a cowboy hustled in.

It was Woolly Buck Rankin, the long-standing foreman of the Star LD ranch. He was a tall rangy jasper in his middle forties sporting a wavy handlebar moustache. Rankin's nickname was an apt label due to his affinity for Angora chaps. He was an experienced cowhand more at home with a lariat and branding iron, as opposed to the recent influx of hands hired for their shooting ability.

That said, he was a loyal employee and came straight to the point. 'The boss wants to know what you're doing about that latest bunch of cattle that have had their brands altered. I told you last week that we spotted them at the auction market in Crown Point.'

'I've been asking around, Woolly. But so far I ain't managed to pin down the culprits,' Lincoln replied evenly. 'But you can assure Mister Devine that I'm doing all I can to track them down. And now I've gotten a reliable deputy, it shouldn't take long before I can make an arrest.'

'We reckon it has to be those damned soddies,' the foreman insisted. 'It's them critters you should be questioning. Only this morning I found some wire had been cut over on the north range.'

'Leave it with me. I'll get Wes here to do some poking around,' the lawman said, calming the ruffled cowpoke down sufficiently to see him out the door with a less aggrieved look marring his weather-beaten face.

As the door closed on the partially satisfied cowpoke, Tate addressed his colleague. 'This is what I'm stuck in the middle of. Devine on one side and those settlers led by a firebrand called Sam Wetherby on the other.' He took out a bottle of whiskey and poured himself a liberal slug. 'It's enough to drive anybody to drink.'

And things were about to become a sight more heated. No more than ten minutes after Rankin had left, another visitor stamped into the office boasting an angry glower. To Wes Longbaugh's jaundiced gaze, the slouch hat and worn dungarees immediately placed him in the sodbuster mould. The two adversaries must have missed each other by a whisker. That was fortunate indeed otherwise big trouble could have flared up, this man being the unofficial leader of the small band of settlers who were at odds with Devine's ruthless ambition to be top dog in the San Miguel Valley.

Wetherby bore an equally furious front as he burst out claiming his well had been poisoned. 'It's that skunk Devine what's done it,' he remonstrated angrily, banging his fist on the desk. 'He's already tried to force me out by fencing off the main water supply for the valley. And this is what happens when I won't play ball.'

Lincoln gave his deputy a jaded look as if to say – 'What was I just saying?' The tin star raised his hands. 'Now calm down, Sam,' he cajoled the grizzled farmer. 'You can't come busting in here throwing accusations about unless you have proof to back them up. You'd be laughed out of court.'

'Who said anything about courts?' Wetherby coughed out a sardonic guffaw that held no shred of humour. 'I know full well it was him. And if'n you won't do something about it, me and the boys sure will. You can bet on it. We won't be pushed around.

Where I come from we don't need your kind of law to get things done. The San Miguel is open range and we have as much right here as anybody else.' He poked a finger in the lawman's chest. 'I'm giving you fair warning, marshal. Sort this out or we will.' And then he stamped out in the same disgruntled manner by which he had entered.

Lincoln shook his head with exasperation. 'On one side there's a ruthless cattle baron, on the other hotheads like Wetherby. Why in thunder do I bother? Sometimes I feel like quitting the whole darned business and letting them fight it out among themselves.'

'But you won't, will you?' Wes posited. 'The only way the West can be made safe for decent folks to live in is for guys like you to bite the bullet and knuckle down. It can be tough work, there's no denying that. In my business I've come across other lawmen who wear that badge with pride, knowing that to abandon it would allow the powers of darkness to take control. And that would be a sad day for America.'

Lincoln arrowed his colleague with a puzzled frown. 'And where do you stand in all this, Wes? Are you gonna side with the bad guys or back us so-called knights in shining armour?'

Wes thought about it. He knew the answer well enough. Nonetheless he left it open. 'I haven't rightly decided yet. Maybe I'm like you . . . caught in the middle.'

'And, as you so wisely pointed out, that is a good place to get trampled on.'

'I'll start by taking a ride out to see Devine on his

95

own territory. See what he has to say. That way I can figure out first hand what sort of threat he poses. Especially now he's taken on Rowdy Bill Hogget.'

NINE

FENCING AROUND

The next day, Wes brought his horse to a standstill outside the limits of the Star LD holding. The ornately gated entrance was meant to impress on visitors the fact that the occupier was a prosperous and successful businessman. A sign in red proclaiming it to be private property was likewise intended to convey the blunt message that any hindrance to the owner's ambitious expansion programme would be dealt with in a ruthless and decisive manner.

As far as the eye could see, a barbed wire fence marked off the boundary as it stood at the present time. Wes harboured no illusion that it would grow larger at the expense of anybody foolish enough to stand in the way of the occupier's self-styled progress. No hesitation was exhibited about ignoring the exclusion directive.

Pushing open the gate, he rode along the clear

track. On all sides cattle were grazing contentedly on the lush grassland. Another half hour passed before a magnificent ranch house hove into view. Even a born cynic such as Wes Longbaugh couldn't help but be enthused by the sumptuous architecture of the place.

Leroy Devine certainly had no inhibitions when it came to living the high life, nor had he spared any expense to flaunt his success. Pointed minarets graced the corner windows on the upper floor, each bearing a flag of the rancher's brand – the Star LD. The man himself was standing on the veranda, a cigar in one hand, a glass in the other. His solid stance was meant to convey intimidating power.

A mean-eyed jasper used to having his orders obeyed without question, Devine cut a solidly candid figure. Wes had come across jaspers of his ilk many times before though never in his current role which felt mighty uncomfortable. But the stoical demeanour gave nothing away as he drew to a halt and dismounted.

Devine was a stocky dude attired in a dark store-bought suit. A thin moustache twitched with amusement on spotting the metal badge of authority. Dark staring eyes hooded beneath beetled brows evoked a coldly piercing appraisal of the newcomer. Wes could feel the man's gaze delving into his soul. He immediately sensed how dangerous this man could be. A flick of his wrist and a dozen hidden guns could take him down with nary a blink of emotion to disturb the flint-eyed masquerade.

It was Devine who broke the impasse. A broad smile, cold as it was menacing, accompanied the deep voiced salutation. 'Glad to see somebody has decided to investigate my complaint regarding that wire cutting,' he almost spat out. 'Although I would have preferred the boss man himself to come out here to sort the matter out rather than his minion.' He sucked on the cigar, puffing out a perfect smoke ring. 'I was a tad surprised when my foreman reported back that the famous gunfighter Wes Longbaugh had taken on the job. A bit out of your line, I would have thought.' His eyebrows lifted questioningly.

Wes returned the snake-eyed smirk with the same deadpan regard. Guys like this did not intimidate him. 'You might wish to know that the marshal is investigating a complaint that you poisoned a well on land occupied by a farmer called Sam Wetherby.'

Devine hawked out a brittle laugh. 'That no account squatter and others of his kind are trespassing on land that rightly belongs to me. That's cattle country and it's been registered to my name. I'm just waiting on verification by the county land agency. I ain't done nothing wrong.'

The vehement denial of any unlawful activity received a bleak response. 'You didn't answer the question, Mister Devine. Did you poison that well?'

'Of course I didn't.' Devine was beginning to lose his cool. The cigar was tossed aside. He jabbed a be-ringed finger at his accuser. 'That critter just wants to stir up trouble among the other gatecrashing sod-busters. Wetherby blames me for everything. He refuses to accept that I was here first and I ain't gonna be pushed out.'

The blustering outburst was soon tempered. The rancher knew that succumbing to histrionics was not the way to deal with this man. Adopting a more conciliatory tone, he said, 'Listen up, Wes. All I want is to bring peace to the San Miguel Valley. Those critters are not making it easy for me.'

'From what I've heard, you have a mighty high-handed way of going about it,' Wes replied.

The accusation was brushed casually aside with another complaint. 'And did I mention they've been rustling my cattle and changing the brands?' Before he had a chance to say any more, a Mexican girl emerged from the house. She immediately came to a halt, eyes wide and staring at the newcomer. Wes's only response to the unexpected interruption was a slight stiffening of the shoulders. Quick to pick up on the ill-concealed magnetism, the phony smile slipped from Devine's face. 'I see that you two are already acquainted.'

The girl remained silently staring at the newcomer. It was Wes who broke the impasse. 'Maria and I are old friends. I helped her out of a rather sticky situation a couple of years back down in El Paso.' The warm smile was reciprocated with a shaky look that hinted of fear, which Wes couldn't help but notice. 'So what brings you to these parts, Maria?'

Devine butted in to provide the answer. 'Maria and I met up while I was over in Denver buying a prize bull. She agreed to come and work as my erm . . .

housekeeper. Isn't that right, my dear?' The snake-like glower told of severe repercussions should the correct answer not be forthcoming.

The girl nodded. 'I am happy to serve Senor Devine,' she trotted out in a leaden delivery, almost as if she had been schooled should such a question ever be asked. 'He treats me well. I have no complaints.' Her beseeching gaze appealed to Wes not to cause any friction.

Wes was in no way hoodwinked by the girl's barely concealed apprehension, but he played along not wanting to cause her any trouble. 'I'm glad to hear it. I wouldn't take kindly to another skunk like Ivory Joe Tanner messing up your life.'

The implied threat received a curt response. 'Maria has nothing to fear from Leroy Devine I can assure you. Now if'n you could get our guest some refreshment, my dear, including those fine cookies you've baked, it would be much appreciated.'

After the girl had retired to the kitchen, Devine got back to business. 'I have big plans for the Star LD, Wes. And those who support me will also benefit hugely from my success. There's also a firm suggestion that the Northern Pacific are all set to push a branch line down here. That would bring enormous prosperity to the valley. But I need men around me I can trust. And I pay well for their loyalty.' He paused, handing Wes a fine Havana cigar and lighting it before adding, 'Would you be interested in joining my organization?'

Wes drew on the cigar, relishing the unique taste

of a quality product. 'I might well be, Mister Devine. It all depends on how much you are prepared to pay?'

'Name your price. Having a man of your reputation at my back will be worth every last dollar.'

'Sounds mighty tempting,' Wes said, giving the appearance that he was seriously considering the generous proposal. 'Reckon at the moment though I'd better see how things pan out in my present job. I need to concentrate on keeping the peace around here. After all, as you so rightly claim, that's what we all want, isn't it? And I don't like going back on my word. I'm sure you understand.'

Wes maintained a straight face, watching as the ruthless tycoon struggled to keep his cool. 'There's nothing I want more. But there are those around here who don't appear to agree with me. And they're making it a mighty tough undertaking.'

The refreshments were served on the veranda. Following some desultory conversation, Devine excused himself when Buck Rankin arrived at the gallop. 'We've gotten some more trouble with fence cutting, boss,' he informed the rancher.

'What did I tell you, deputy,' Devine sighed, not bothering to conceal his burning irritation.

'This is what I'm having to deal with on a daily basis. You finish your cigar and have another brandy. This won't take long to sort out.'

'Just so long as what you have in mind is within the law,' Wes said, making sure the devious landowner knew he could not be bought.

Devine scowled then stepped down off the veranda, following his foreman over behind the barn out of earshot. As soon as her employer had disappeared, Maria emerged from the ranch house. 'You must leave now, Wes. There is much danger for you here. Devine, he plan to take over whole valley by force. Stand in his way and he will have you killed.'

She was still urging him to leave the valley when Devine spotted the conflab from across the yard. Although he did not hear what was being said, it was clear from the girl's heartfelt body language that this was no mundane exchange of pleasantries. 'Get back to your work, girl,' he snapped out brusquely. 'And don't come back until you are called.'

Wes's whole body tensed. He was about to voice a brittle objection when the girl gripped his arm, silently imploring him to hold his tongue. Without another word, she lowered her head, collected up the crockery and departed meekly.

'Guess I'll be moseying along,' Wes declared, as if nothing untoward had just taken place. Yet inside he was fuming knowing what critters such as Devine were capable of when crossed.

'You think hard on what's in your best interests, deputy. The alternative might prove costly.' Wes gave no indication that he had heard the implied threat as he rode away.

Inside the bunkhouse, Rowdy Bill Hogget had been watching the exchange with mounting vexation. He would have dearly loved to call this man out there and then. Neither had met before but each knew that the reputation amassed by the other was well earned. Had Hogget known about the offer from Devine he might well have ignored any orders to lie low; Rowdy Bill always had to be top dog. Another renowned gunslinger on the payroll was a step too far.

As things stood, he merely arrowed daggers of hate towards the gunfighter's back. A silent promise hinted that one day soon a showdown would most assuredly follow. So Wes Longbaugh had decided to change sides, now that was a turn up for the books. Sure it had happened before. Guys who lived by the gun often climbed over the fence if and when the need arose. Bill Hickok immediately sprang to mind.

A lascivious gleam shone in Hogget's black gaze while lovingly fondling the well-oiled six-shooter in his hand. Now there was a critter he would dearly love to take down. While marshal of Abilene the skunk had shot his best pal. Dakota Red Stabler hadn't stood a chance.

The bitter recollection was interrupted by Buck Rankin. 'Boss wants to see you over at the house,' the foreman declared. 'And he's looking mighty peeved since that new deputy arrived.' The grizzled cowpoke had little time for the new breed of men his boss had brought in. Sure as hell they weren't cattlemen, merely bodyguards here to ensure things went smoothly to further the ranch owner's territorial ambitions.

Things were heading in a direction that made Buck Rankin distinctly uneasy. So far he had kept his mouth shut. His loyalty stemmed from their time in the war while attached to the 21st Indiana Foot. Ex-major Devine had saved his sergeant from certain death when a rebel bayonet was about to skewer him in the guts.

Following the Confederate surrender, the two had headed back to Texas, where Devine had taken over his deceased father's cattle empire. With the Northern cities demanding fresh beef on the hoof, there was a lot of money to be made by astute and enterprising ranchers. Devine had proved himself to be one of the most successful, and that achievement had rubbed off onto his old comrade.

A lowly cow punching job for his loyal sergeant had soon led to him becoming the major's right-hand man. Everything had been going smoothly until Devine decided to sell up in Texas and move to Colorado. And there the rot had set in. Ruthless ambition began to cast its ugly shadow over fair dealings.

At first Buck had gone along with the major's plans for expansion, but there was only so far that a man could stretch his allegiance. The threatened range war in the San Miguel Valley had become the straw that might well break the camel's back, yet abandonment of his old commanding officer felt like a betrayal of trust akin to desertion. He was not yet ready for such a drastic move.

So Woolly Buck merely scowled at the latest recruit's strutting gait and carried on with his regular duties.

TEN

BARBED WIRE
BUST-UP

A good night's sleep had eluded Wes Longbaugh.
The skirmish with Leroy Devine had left a nasty taste
in the mouth. The one good thing to come out of the
encounter was meeting up with Maria Elena. Theirs
had been a fleeting courtship that was never going to
flourish, such was the nature of being a hired gunfighter, although on seeing her after all this time, he
grasped that the Mexican girl still had amorous feelings for him. It was an unsettling notion, prompting
his concern as to how much of a hold Devine had
over her.

In the not too distant past he would have had no
qualms about backing the rancher's hand. Money
talked in those days. Any scruples he might have harboured finished a poor second to that of enhancing
his credentials for getting the job done and collect-

ing his thirty pieces of silver. It was true that he had never deliberately broken the law, merely bent it to suit his own motives.

All that had changed since coming into contact with Mace Farlow, not to mention the delectable Kay Lincoln and her affable father. His sense of right and wrong had shifted somewhat onto a more altruistic level. Could it be that he was acquiring a conscience? His old buddies would be aghast, appalled that the infamous Wes Longbaugh had defected to the other side.

He rolled over on the bed, studying the five-pointed star attached to his vest. A tentative finger traced around the outline, his mind still undecided as to which side of the fence he had actually fallen. Outside his window the creak of wagons rolling along the street informed him that the new day was well under way. Dogs were barking; children laughing on their way to the schoolhouse.

Cold water splashed over a stubble-coated face helped bring the sparkle back into the leaden gaze he perceived in the mirror. After deftly removing the dark coating of fuzz with a cut-throat razor, he almost felt like his old self. Settling his vest on broad shoulders, he buffed the metal star, still uncertain as to which fork in the trail he should follow. Without thinking, he buckled on the gunbelt, settling it comfortably round his waist with the sheath knife on the opposite side.

A grumbling in his stomach told him that the inner man required sustenance that involved eggs and bacon washed down with a pot of hot Arbuckles. However, the much anticipated breakfast would have to wait.

On descending the stairs, Wes was brought to a halt by a measured yet insistent discussion taking place in the lobby between two men, one of whom he recognized as the sodbuster Sam Wetherby. It was the other man referred to as Griff who was grumbling about two wagons loaded up with barbed wire parked in the street outside. 'Devine has gotten some nerve bringing that stuff into town. He's asking for trouble rubbing our noses in the trough like that.'

His friend responded with a thin-lipped smile. Griff Teale looked around to ensure nobody was within earshot. Had he looked up he would have spotted the figure of Wes Longbaugh about to descend the stairs. 'There's only a couple of hands guarding it. Seems to me this is the ideal chance for us to snatch the lot and dump it in that ravine outside town. What do you say? Should I get the others? They're waiting in the Broken Bottle saloon at the north end of town.'

Wetherby was a tad hesitant. 'What about Lincoln?' he posited, rubbing his pointed chin thoughtfully. 'He ain't gonna stand idly by when gunfire breaks out. And it'll be us what takes the blame.'

'Not if'n he ain't around,' Teale replied slyly. 'I had one of the boys send him on a wild goose chase out to Dead Man's Bluff to investigate an abandoned wagon. That should keep him busy long enough for what I have in mind.'

Wetherby's eyes lit up. 'Then what are we waiting for. You gather up the boys and I'll meet you down China Alley in fifteen minutes.' He rubbed his hands. 'This will sure wipe the slimy grin off'n Devine's face.'

'He'll know then that us little guys ain't gonna roll over and eat dirt,' Teale added. As soon as the two conspirators had left the hotel, Wes also left, hustling across the street to where the two guards were standing beside the wagons. 'You the only fellas guarding this stuff?' he asked.

The two cowpokes tensed, looking him over. 'What business is that of your'n, mister?' one of them rasped.

Wes tapped his badge of authority. 'I'm the new deputy marshal. So it's my job to prevent a crime that's about to be committed.'

'What you talking about?' the other man enquired.

'If'n you turkeys don't get some help pronto, these wagons will be stolen,' Wes emphasized. 'Where are the rest of your hands?'

'They're waiting down by the river crossing,' said the first man.

'Then go get them quick before the fun starts.' The two men looked at each other unsure what to do. Wes replied with a caustic retort. 'If'n you don't want to feel Devine's wrath, I suggest one of you shifts his damned ass right now.'

'I'll gather up Rondo and Fletch Akker,' a puncher by the name of Elko Sager declared, hurrying off. 'They're playing faro in the Cow Palace over yonder. You keep your eyes peeled until we get back.'

While Sager was hurrying off across the street, Wes retired to the far side, concealing his bulky frame behind some barrels of tar oil to keep watch on developments. He didn't have long to wait because Devine's men soon arrived, and there they huddled behind the wagons, guns drawn ready to repel the threatened ambush.

A flurry of movement in China Alley told the hidden deputy that Wetherby and his supporters were about to make their presence felt. Stuck in the middle, Wes knew he needed to defuse the imminent fracas before it blew up with dire results. Narrow eyes flicked between the two factions.

Before he could decide how best to stop the shoot-out, Wetherby called out, 'OK boys, let the skunks have it.' Orange tongues of flame immediately spat out from the alleyway as the bushwhackers emerged from hiding.

'Drop your weapons,' Wes called out.

But he was too late; the order was drowned out by the hail of gunfire from both sides. The deputy knew he had to act fast to avert a certain bloodbath. Fortune favours the brave and luck was on his side in the form of three steel balls overhanging the alley that advertised the pawnbroker business of Ezekial Patternoster. Without a second thought, he brought the Colt revolver up, pumping three shells at the narrow pins securing the heavy silver balls.

Each found its mark, and down they tumbled. One cracked Wetherby on the head, stunning him, while the other two startled his comrades sufficiently for them to terminate their gun play. The surprise with which they had hoped to defeat their adversaries was well and truly kiboshed. 'Now drop them hoglegs pronto,' Wes repeated decisively. So that all participants understood the alternative to compliance, he stepped out in full view of the assailants, 'Or else the next call will be for an undertaker.'

Rather than submit to the ignominy of being marched over to the jailhouse, Griff Teale hauled his stupefied buddy to his feet and, along with the others, disappeared down the alley. Wes judged it wise to let them go. One against five in a confined space was asking too much even for him to survive. He sauntered across to where the ranch hands were milling about.

Elko Sager voiced what the others were all thinking. 'Gee, I ain't never seen shooting like that before.'

'Who in tarnation are you, mister,' his sidekicker muttered.

'I'm the man who has been hired to help bring peace to Saw Tooth and the San Miguel Valley. And anybody who objects will answer to my friend here, the Equalizer.' He spun the nickel-plated six shooter on his middle finger and, with a deliberate flourish intended to impress, slipped it back into the holster. 'Now you best go tell that boss of your'n that what

Wes Longbaugh says goes for him as well.'

Leaving the astounded cowpokes open-mouthed, he then marched down the middle of the street. His destination was the Broken Bottle saloon, where he reckoned Sam Wetherby and his cowed minions would be gathering to lick their wounds. Unlike the appropriately named Cow Palace, which was the sole preserve of cattle men, the Broken Bottle was a much humbler establishment with little in the way of luxurious fittings. No lurid paintings of scantily clad sirens adorned the walls, just a few faded Indian blankets. This was solely a drinking den for sodbusters.

Wes entered the austere saloon without any hesitation. Through the smoke-laden atmosphere he perceived four rough-clad nesters leaning on the bar supping tin mugs of beer. They were so busy discussing the failure of their recent debacle that the newcomer escaped notice. Only when a bunched fist was banged on the bar top did they deign to look up.

'I said for you to shuck those weapons. Now do it!' he spelled out in a flat tone. 'You can collect them when you leave town.' That was when he noticed their self-appointed leader was absent. 'Where's that big mouth, Sam Wetherby? I guess he must be skulking out back rubbing the sore head I gave him.'

The thoroughly cowed group were about to comply when the man in question pushed them aside and stepped forward into view. And he was none too pleased. His face was flushed with anger, having just fastened a bandage over the gash inflicted by the pawn ball. 'So it was you that did this, was it mister?'

Wes responded with a blunt threat. 'And I'll do it again if'n you give me cause.'

'You've gotten a darned nerve coming in here large as life ordering us about. It's them Star CD rannies you should be hassling, not us.' Wetherby stepped forward, jabbing a finger at the lawman. 'All we want is to farm our sections in peace.'

'Taking the law into your own hands ain't the answer,' Wes snapped. 'And neither is luring the marshal out of town so's you can start a danged range war. There'll be no vigilante law in Saw Tooth while I'm wearing this badge.' He tapped the star purposefully. 'Now are you gonna surrender them guns or do I have to arrest you for disturbing the peace.'

Wetherby scoffed. 'Figure you can run us all down to the hoosegow, deputy?' Sniggers could be heard behind as the recently browbeaten nesters began to regain their lost nerve. 'What do you reckon, boys? Only in town two minutes and this guy acts like he owns the place. He ain't gonna make many friends by throwing in with Devine and his crew of land grabbers.'

'You trying to threaten me, fella?' The thin-lipped grimace should have warned Sam Wetherby that he was venturing into turbulent waters.

'Well I sure ain't inviting you to the next barn dance.' Chuckles greeted this gem of witticism from their strutting leader.

Another finger was about to jab Wes in the chest when Wetherby suddenly found his arm being twisted up his back and a gun barrel tapping his cheekbone. 'I don't cotton to guys that treat the law like it don't affect them,' he growled. 'The rest of you boys put your guns on the bar for safe keeping. This turnip cruncher is gonna be spending the night in a nice uncomfortable cell. But at least he'll have the cockroaches for company,' Wes declared, dragging the captive towards the door of the saloon. 'It'll cost you a ten dollar fine to get him released.'

The new deputy's face split in a broad grin of satisfaction as the bartender went around the saloon commandeering all the hardware. 'You won't get away with this, deputy,' Wetherby railed impotently. 'We'll sort you out one way or another.'

'Seems like I already have, Sam.' A gentle tap from the gun barrel reminded the nester that he was the prisoner. 'And that piece of abuse has cost you another five dollars. You fellas have thirty minutes to drink up and leave town. I wouldn't want to be in your shoes when Marshal Lincoln gets back from that wild goose chase. Wasting a lawman's time is a serious offence.' He shrugged nonchalantly. 'Not that I mind seeing as how I earn a cut of all fines collected.'

With the tricky situation nicely turned in his favour, Wes marched the subdued captive over to the jailhouse. Wetherby was further humiliated by having to pass the two wagons he and his buddies were hoping to hijack and destroy. The Hardacre boys had been watching the fracas from a safe place below the raised veranda. Now that the fun was over they emerged to congratulate the famous gunslinging deputy.

'That sure was some fancy shooting, Mister Longbaugh,' Tommy gushed, full of awe.

'Take note, kid, that I defused a tricky situation without a single drop of blood being split,' Wes declared proudly. 'That's the reason guys that wear the badge are called peace officers.'

'What about this bandage round my head,' grumbled Wetherby.

'That don't count,' Wes rapped. 'Now shut your trap else there'll be no supper for you tonight.'

Around an hour later, Marshal Lincoln was returning somewhat puzzled from his fruitless investigation when he came upon the sodbusters heading back to their holdings. He signalled for them to draw rein. 'What was all that about an abandoned wagon at Dead Man's Bluff? I couldn't find anything there.'

Teale quickly concocted a suitable reply. 'Some fella passing through town told us about it. Guess he must have been mistaken.' Vigorous nods from the others supported the culprit, who shrugged his shoulders while praying silently that his weak excuse would be believed. 'All I did was pass on the message. Sorry you had a wasted journey, marshal.'

'So am I,' Lincoln huffed, none too pleased but ready to accept the excuse. 'I don't like having my time wasted.' A curt flick of the head told the grateful riders to be on their way. They did not linger, relieved that no action had been taken by the suspicious lawman. The fact that it was only delaying matters did not occur to them.

When Lincoln arrived back in Saw Tooth he went immediately to the jail, where he found his daughter anxiously enquiring after the new deputy's health. 'I heard all the shooting and came right over to see if you had been injured.' Surprised but pleased about the girl's concern for his welfare, Wes was more than ready to bathe in her approbation.

'Knowing that your pa here had been lured away like that, I knew that swift action was needed to avoid a full scale shoot-out,' he replied, trying to play down any heroic connotation Kay Lincoln might be harbouring. 'I didn't agree to wear this badge to stand aside when trouble comes calling. So it was up to me to sort it out.'

'So Griff Teale was pulling the wool over my eyes,' the aggrieved marshal rumbled. 'That tale he spun sounded mighty fishy but at the time I met them on the trail, there was no reason to doubt his openness.' Then he scratched his thinning pate. 'Now I come to think on it, there was no sign of the ring leader.'

Wes slung a thumb towards the cell block. 'He's cooling his heels in there with a sore head.' Wes went on to relate the tricky circumstances leading to the leader of the sodbusters getting himself locked up.

Kay gripped his arm on learning the dicey facts of how he had single-handedly thwarted the ambush. Wes had no objections to enjoying her closeness, especially the alluring smell of pure woman wafting from her floating tresses.

It was Lincoln who brought his deputy's thoughts

back to the problem in hand. 'My figuring is that
Devine is behind this,' he suggested. 'He deliberately
left those wagons in town to rile the nesters and
encourage them to steal it. He was probably waiting
down by the creek ford with his men ready to mount
his own ambush then claim he was only protecting
his property.' The lawman's hooded eyes narrowed.
'That's the type of devious varmint we're dealing
with here.' He patted Wes on the shoulder. 'Boy, it
sure was my lucky day when you hit town. Don't
reckon I could have handled this alone.'

A coy smile from Kay concurred with that view.
The girl's reservations concerning his motives
appeared to have dissolved, and Wes sure wasn't
about to question that. All the same, he had been left
in no doubt that, like the marshal had said, uphold-
ing the law left him walking a fine line. It was one
that would require all his skill to avoid getting trampled on by both factions.

'I'll go check that those wagons are removed from
town,' he said. 'Looks like you need to rest up, Tate,
after all that running around like a headless
chicken.'

The marshal yawned. There was no denial there.
Suddenly he felt his age catching up. 'I'll check on
Sam, then I'll get me some shuteye,' he said. 'The
guy is a hot head but he has good reason to be angry.
Reckon we shouldn't be too hard on those fellas.'

Wes remained non-committal as he stepped
outside. Those sodbusters had been all set to start a
war on the streets of Saw Tooth. He was walking

across with the intention of instructing the cowboys to remove the offending wagons when he was intercepted by the Star LD boss himself. Devine was all grateful smiles. 'Much obliged to you, deputy, for stopping those nesters from stealing my barbed wire.'

Wes ignored the unctuous praise. 'Those wagons should never have been in town in the first place. It was asking for trouble. A suspicious man might be inclined to think it was a deliberate ploy to hoodwink Wetherby and the other farmers.'

The smile slipped from Devine's rubicund features. 'You accusing me of setting a trap? I trust you have proof of that.'

'Just saying what others might be thinking is all,' came back the ambiguous reply. 'Now get those wagons off the street.'

Devine stiffened. 'I don't cotton to anybody ordering me about,' he rasped, trying to control a bubbling temper. 'Your high-handed attitude appears to imply that you're turning down my generous offer? A foolish decision, deputy. One that could prove costly.'

Wes fixed a gimlet eye onto the arrogant landowner. 'Certainly not for me. So who you gonna take your anger out on, Mister Devine? That young Mexican girl? I wouldn't take kindly to hearing she's been wronged in any way.'

Devine threw down his cigar and stamped hard on it to vent his feeling that this man was much shrewder than he had previously assumed. 'Guess we

118

know where we stand then.'

'Guess we do at that,' Wes replied casually as he turned his back on the seething rancher and walked away. 'You have thirty minutes to get those wagons out of town or they'll be impounded.'

ELEVEN

ROWDY DISTURBANCE

The next day around midday, a lone rider approached the Wetherby cabin. After tethering his horse outside he knocked on the door and waited. It was Charlotte Wetherby who answered the door. A drawn face, lined and pitted, due to the relentless grind of eking a meagre living from the soil, peered at the stranger. 'Can I help you, sir?' she enquired amiably.

The man smiled back, but somehow the gesture lacked any warmth. 'Just passing by, ma'am,' he said tipping his hat. 'I saw your cabin and wondered if'n you would fill up my canteen. It's down to the last few drops.'

'Who's there, Charlotte?' a voice from inside the cabin called out. Sam Wetherby was just about to

120

commence his meal.

'Just a stranger asking for some water, Sam,' his wife replied.

'Then ask him in, woman. We don't get many visitors out here,' the nester replied, getting to his feet. He greeted the newcomer warmly, holding out a hand that the stranger accepted. 'Sit down and join us for dinner. The food's simple fare but Charlotte's a good cook. Can I pour you some home-made beer?'

'That's mighty kind of you folks,' the man replied, removing his hat, the frosty grin still pasted to his stubble-coated face. 'I always say that a man can't go wrong eating home-cooked chow.' He looked around the room as the food was ladled out. 'You keep a mighty fine house, ma'am. Being a single man I can't help but be envious of you, Mister Wetherby.'

The newcomer was about to tuck in when Wetherby stopped him. 'Being God-fearing folks, we always say grace before a meal, stranger.' The man apologized and dutifully bowed his head as the blessing of the food was espoused.

While the meal was consumed, the conversation followed a general pattern regarding news from the outside world. Farmers living in remote frontier settlements rarely had the opportunity to question incomers. Sam Wetherby was no different. Inevitably the conversation came round to the stranger's reason for passing through the San Miguel Valley. 'You looking for work, mister?' he asked, offering the last slice of apple pie to their guest. The man nodded his appreciation as Sam added, 'There's always plenty available in the logging camps.'

'Nope,' came back the casual reply as the stranger wiped the crumbs from his face. 'I already have a job.' Sam's eyes lifted, a gesture urging the man to enlighten them. He paused wiping his lips before addressing Charlotte. 'That was a mighty fine meal, Mrs. Wetherby. Best I've tasted in a long while.'

The woman coloured at the compliment, looking away modestly. The man's polite manner, however, had blurred the frosty glint of his gaze. In contrast, Sam had picked up on another rather unsettling conundrum. 'How come you know our name, mister? I never mentioned it.' The warm smile had slipped from his face.

'Perhaps that's because my boss told me to deliver a message especially for you good folks,' the man casually revealed. 'You see I'm working for an important man around here who runs the Star LD cattle ranch. You might have heard of it.'

All of a sudden, a macabre chill settled over the gathering. 'You're working for that land-grabbing skunk, Devine?' Sam blurted out, barely able to grasp the implications of this visit. Charlotte gripped his arm, urging her hot-tempered husband to calm down. But the nester was angered by this man's blatant effrontery. 'You come into my house, eat my food and tell me . . . well, what exactly are you here for?'

'The fact is, Mister Wetherby,' the man said, keeping the creepy smile in place. 'You're trespassing. Simple as that. This is Star LD land and you have

twenty-four hours to vacate the premises.' He casually picked up the knife recently used to cut meat
and tested the blade for sharpness. Then, without
any warning, he stabbed the point into the wooden
table, ripping a hole in the white cloth.

The abrupt display of aggression drew a choking
cry from Charlotte Wetherby. More outraged than
frightened, Sam growled, 'Why you sneaky rat, you
can't do that. This is open range and we've occupied
it under the Homestead Act.' Without waiting for any
devious excuses to the contrary, Sam lunged at their
uninvited house guest.

But the inept move was easily parried by the
intruder, who grabbed the outstretched hand. 'Now
that was a foolish mistake, Mister Wetherby. Very
foolish. One that deserves a lesson in obedience. All
the other settlers I've visited today have been persuaded that leaving is in their best interest. I'm
disappointed that you are choosing to be difficult.'
He shook his head in mock admonition.

Then, fastening a ghoulishly staring eye onto the
farmer, a quick downward thrust and the sharp
blade pinned the offending limb to the table. Sam's
mouth opened in stunned shock as he gaped disbe-
lievingly at his pinioned hand oozing blood.
Charlotte screamed but remained glued to her
chair in abject terror. The sadistic invader merely
smiled back. Slowly he rose to his feet and walked
across to the dresser by the door. Sam gasped aloud
as the pain hit him. His wife mewed like a scalded
cat.

The bloodthirsty intruder gently picked up a blue-patterned plate and nodded. 'A very nice piece. You have good taste, Mrs Wetherby.' Then he let it fall to shatter on the floor. 'But I don't think you'll have enough room in a wagon to take all the others with you.' And with that indictment, he tipped the dresser and all its contents over. The whole caboodle crashed into a myriad bits of smashed crockery.

More petrified howling emerged from Charlotte's throat.

'Twenty-four hours, remember. Or my next visit will not be so pleasant.' The macabre grin was still pasted across his cold-blooded facade. He turned to leave, then paused. 'I'm forgetting my manners. I should have introduced myself. The name is Hogget. Some folks call me Rowdy Bill. I can't think why.' Then he drew his pistol, causing the terrified duo to shrink back. 'I think your husband needs some attention, ma'am. He'll need to be fit and well for the coming journey.' The gun blasted a figurine, leaving a much cherished heirloom as a distant memory.

Again Charlotte screamed. Yet far from being cowed, her brutalized husband somehow managed to find his voice and conjured up a spirited if powerless resistance. Holding back the agonizing barbs lancing through his hand, a final challenge emerged as a hoarse warning. 'Marshal Lincoln ain't gonna stand by and let this happen,' he gasped out. 'You tell Devine he can't ride rough shod over honest hardworking folks like us.'

The cutting invective caused the hard-bitten

gunman to revert to type. A snarled twist of fury replaced the frosty smile. The gun swung towards the farmer. 'You ain't been listening, mister,' he rasped. 'Maybe I should finish you off here and now.' Then he shrugged, once again assuming that more sinister, yet disturbing persona. 'But I'm a fella who obeys the instructions from my employer. You got twenty-four hours. No more, no less. Use that time well to think on the alternative.'

Once again he turned to leave. 'And that tin star ain't gonna help you,' he said hawking out a gruesome laugh. 'Not when I've finished with him. That's where I'll be heading next after I've reported back to the boss that you good people won't be causing him any more bother.'

Then he was gone, leaving a totally distraught Charlotte Wetherby to gently prise her pain-wracked husband free of his torment. 'What we gonna do, Sam?' she wailed, tending the bleeding injury.

'I ain't giving up without a fight, Charlotte,' he asserted firmly.

His wife had seen that determined cast often enough before and feared the worst. 'That man means what he says. Stay here and he'll come back and likely burn us out, then shoot us down. You ain't no gunfighter, Sam,' his wife pleaded. 'Nor are any of the others. And what can you do with a useless hand? Devine is too darned powerful for the likes of us.'

The sodbuster waved aside her protestations. 'If'n we all stand together, there's a better chance of holding him off.' His mind was made up and nothing would change it save a bullet in the head. Charlotte's tormented expression clearly expressed her fear that such an outcome was more than a distinct possibility. 'Soon as you've bandaged me up, I'm heading over to see Griff Teale.' When his wife tried one last time to urge caution, Sam cut her off by raising the injured hand. 'We can't allow scum like that to do this and drive us off land we're entitled to farm, woman.'

From the doggedly determined glint in his eye and vehement exclamation, Charlotte knew better than to argue further. When Sam got the bit between his teeth nothing would sway him. Slowly she began to tidy up the mess left by the vicious gunman. It felt like a hurricane had passed through her home. All she could do now was hope and pray.

It was not until the next day that Sam Wetherby managed to bring enough nesters around to his way of thinking. They had all experienced a visit from Bill Hogget, together with his uniquely destructive sting in the tail. But Sam's fervent entreaty helped to strength their backbones. They arrived in Saw Tooth just as Tate Lincoln was opening up the office for the day.

The lawman frowned as the deputation of sod-busters gathered round. 'What's this all about, Sam?' he asked, drawing himself up to face the line of dis-mayed faces. 'I let you off with a fine after that last fracas you started. There better not be any more trouble else I won't be so lenient next time.'

'Why do you think we've come to see you,

marshal?' Sam replied as he followed the lawman inside the office. 'That gunslinger Devine has hired came round yesterday threatening us all if'n we didn't quit the valley today.' He held up the blood-stained bandage. 'This is what I got for standing up for my rights. The guy's a maniac and he's coming here to make sure there ain't no law to stop Devine having his way. We wanna know what you're going to do about it?' Behind their verbose spokesman, the others were avidly nodding their agreement.

Lincoln's whole body stiffened. 'You're saying that Rowdy Bill Hogget is coming here for a showdown?'

'That's what he threatened,' Wetherby averred.

The lawman's eyes narrowed to thin slits as he began buckling on his gunbelt. So it had come down to this. He had always feared a day like this would come soon when Leroy Devine started flexing his muscles. 'You fellas go over to the Broken Bottle and wait there,' he said, trying to keep his voice steady. 'And don't show yourselves until this is over. If'n Hogget wants a showdown, then he's come to the right place.'

Teale was not so sure. 'You taking on Hogget alone, marshal?' he pressed. 'I heard tell that guy is faster than a striking rattler.'

'So is Tate Lincoln. I can handle a no-account like Hogget.' The words were delivered boldly and con-vincing to all save the man who uttered them. But Tate was not about to display any sign of hesitation. These men were farmers, depending on him to save their livelihoods. He waved the gathering away. 'Now go across to the saloon like I said.'

He was checking the load on his Colt Frontier when his daughter pushed through the crowd of nesters who were trouping out of the office. 'That father of your'n sure is one brave fella, ma'am,' one of the nesters enthused, shaking his head. 'I sure wouldn't want to go up against a critter like Bill Hogget.'

Shock and alarm turned Kay Lincoln's smooth features white as snow. She had only arrived to deliver her father's breakfast to be informed that he planned to go up against the hardened gunfighter. Her obvious distress was written in bold across the ashen countenance. 'You can't do this, Pa. He'll kill you for sure.'

Lincoln brushed off the girl's concern. 'This is my job, girl. It's what the town pays me for. I can't just walk away when the going gets tough.'

'But that's the reason you hired Wes Longbaugh,' she protested urgently. 'To help deliver a peaceful life for all in the San Miguel Valley.'

'Maybe so. But I can't ask a man to do my dirty work for me,' he countered bluntly, tying down the thong of his holster. 'The town is looking to me for deliverance. And I aim to give it them.'

His mind was made up. Kay could see that no amount of verbal persuasion was going to change the stubborn old goat's mind. There was only one person who could do that, and he was over at the hotel. She had spotted him going into the National on her way down the street. Without further ado, she left her mule-headed kin and hurried across the street. Once inside the lobby, she took the stairs two at a time and padded along the corridor.

No thought was given as to what she might encounter as she pushed open the door and went into Wes's room. And there another shock greeted her; Wes was not alone. Indeed, he had been caught at a decidedly embarrassing moment in the company of Maria Elena. The Mexican girl had the shoulder straps of her dress undone. What they were about to do appeared obvious and left the interloper stunned and hurt.

Wes was as startled as Kay by her interruption and desperately tried to distance himself from the obvious assumption. Stuttering like a kid caught with his fingers in the cookie jar, he muttered something about this not being what it appeared. 'You got this all wrong, Kay,' he beseeched, stepping away from the girl, who was in no way fazed by the intrusion. Indeed she was smiling. 'Maria has run away from Devine because he's been ill-treating her,' Wes stuttered out in a somewhat lame manner, unable to keep the guilt from his face. 'She came to me for help. All I was doing was looking at her bruises.'

But Kay's scornful regard told him that she did not believe a word. Struggling to keep hold of her dignity, she snorted, 'It makes no difference to me how you choose to spend your free time, or who with.' But the withering glare aimed at the other girl told a different tale entirely. She was deeply distraught. 'I only came across because Bill Hogget is on his way to town and he intends calling Pa out.' Staggered by two separate calamities, the angst-ridden girl burst into tears. 'He's too darned mule-headed to ask for your help.'

Wes hurried across and attempted to comfort her. But the damage had been done. She was having none of that. 'Don't come near me.' The cutting rebuke saw her aiming a final retort at the object of her wrath. 'Go back to your precious Maria. She obviously means far more to you than I ever could.' And with that final rebuff she flounced out of the door.

As Wes made to go after her, Maria attempted to stop him. 'She no good for you, Wesley. Were we not good once back in El Paso? And it could be same again.' She pulled at his shirt, urging him to stay. But the deputy had become totally smitten by Kay Lincoln and pushed her away.

'That was in the past, Maria,' he said. 'You can stay here until I arrange transport for you out of Saw Tooth, but my duty lies elsewhere now.' He was thinking about Tate Lincoln's foolhardy gesture. That had to take priority over any burgeoning feelings he had for Kay.

After rushing out into the corridor, Kay hurried back down the stairs and out of the hotel, struggling to contain her emotions. A growing expectation, hope even, that more than friendship could have developed between her and Wes had been cruelly dashed. It was clear that he and the Mexican girl already knew each other and intended to resurrect an old liaison. What other explanation could there be for a man holding a woman in that way?

She hid her tear-streaked face to avoid any passers-by gaining a hint of her anguish. The last thing she needed now was sympathetic triteness that would become the talk of the local gossips. Although they had barely known each other more than a few days, she felt a distinct attraction had mushroomed between them. Clearly she had badly misread the situation; it was an illusion and nothing more.

Before entering the jailhouse, Kay settled herself into a calmer frame of mind. Her father was in peril of throwing his life away for the sake of foolish masculine pride. Saving him from a wasted death had to take priority over any misguided amorous attraction for a notorious gunslinger. A haughty sniff brushed away such a silly daydream. Whatever had she been thinking?

TWELVE

SHOWDOWN SHELVED . . .

When Wes arrived at the jailhouse, Kay was once again urging her father not to go up against the deadly gunman. She gave the deputy a look of lofty disdain, not stooping to acknowledge his presence. Wes couldn't help but pick up on the strained atmosphere, but he forced it out of his mind, concentrating on backing her intense assertion. 'Your daughter is right, Tate,' he said. 'You wouldn't stand a chance against a hardened gunman like Hogget. He'd drop you afore you had time to draw.'

'You might not know it, young fella, but I've cleaned up more towns in the west than you've had hot dinners.' The stubborn lawman was clearly not about to submit to the law of commonsense easily. A prickly sigh issued from between gritted teeth. At least on this issue the deputy and Kay Lincoln could agree. 'Ain't no way I'm backing down to a scumbag like that. The town expects me to protect them and I intend to carry out my duty come what may.'

The claim was decisive and Wes had no doubts concerning its veracity. But nevertheless, he had no intentions of allowing the ageing starpacker to throw his life away for a common gunman like Rowdy Bill Hogget. 'You're a sight older now, Tate,' he declared, effecting a softer more conciliatory approach. 'Age slows a man down. You don't realize it until too late. Gunfighting is a young man's game. I've seen too many good men heading down the road you're fixed on taking.'

'Listen to what Wes is saying, Pa,' Kay exhorted, apprehension for her father's safety etching deep lines of worry across her distressed features. 'Isn't that why you took him on in the first place?' But Tate was not listening. Nothing, it appeared, would influence him.

Yet still Wes Longbaugh tried. One last attempt was made to drive some rational judgment into the marshal's one-track mind. 'If'n you do intend going out there alone, then take one of these.' He took down a double-barrelled shotgun from the rack and handed it to the bull-headed marshal. 'Nothing says you have to play this critter at his own game, and nobody would think any the worse of you for challenging him out there on your own terms.' He pressed the lethal scatter gun into the lawman's hands. 'Go down in a hail of bullets and it'll just become the tittle-tattle of drunks and gossips before fading into obscurity. And who'll be left to pick up the pieces?' His eyes shifted towards the girl's tear-stained face.

Tate peered down at the gun clutched in his hands, looking somewhat bemused. The single-minded dedication to follow a pre-ordained yet doomed scenario appeared to be fading. The obtuse stoicism evident in his blunt features faded to a hollow gauntness. Sound judgement prescribed by his daughter and this enigmatic newcomer coupled with a blunt realization of the futility of pursuing a death wish appeared to have finally won through.

'Guess you're right, Wes,' the marshal declared. 'I ain't no spring chicken, that's for sure. And who cares about what a few scared citizens think. It's what those I care about think that matters.' Kay breathed a sigh a relief, her heartfelt gaze settling on the man who had penetrated her father's rhino-skinned exterior. The uncomfortable incident in Wes's room appeared to have been shelved, at least for the time being.

Wes hustled over to the window. 'I'll keep you covered from here. But my figuring is that he won't go up against a man brandishing a scatter gun. It would be against the grain and do his reputation no good. If'n he does try any funny business, then it's my duty as your deputy to step in and help out.'

The tense atmosphere of moments before had eased noticeably. A dangerous situation still had to be faced, but at least now there was a good chance of the defender emerging unharmed with his standing in the community still untarnished.

Silence descended over the office as the three of them watched and waited. It was a difficult time for them all. Outside, the town went about its normal business unaware of the imminent showdown. Only those sodbusters huddling in the Broken Bottle had any notion that Saw Tooth's peace and tranquillity was under threat. As the clock on the office wall ticked off the minutes, so the tension again mounted.

Then it happened. The bubble burst as people began leaving the street. Where moments before folks had been hustling to and fro, now there was nobody. Wes narrowed his gaze, focussing on the far end of the main street. 'He's here, Tate.' He opened the door, at the same time palming his Colt .45. 'Take it slow and easy. No quick moves to spook him. I don't need to tell you what to say. No doubt you've faced off more than enough troublemakers before. And I'll be here to back your play. Let's hope I won't be needed.'

Tate Lincoln gave a curt nod and stepped out to face his destiny. His legs felt like lead as he moved slowly into the middle of the street, measuring each step. A man alone, white knuckles clutching the shotgun across his chest, he shook off the nervous tremor gripping his innards and breathed deep. It was a long time since he had stood up against a rabid gunslinger of Hogget's ilk. And standing there he felt like a Christian thrown into the arena to face a battle-scarred gladiator.

As his adversary slowly drew nearer, Tate drew himself up and slammed the gun butt into his shoulder. 'That's far enough, Hogget,' he called out, imbuing as much aggression into the order as he could muster. 'Your kind ain't welcome in Saw Tooth. Turn around and ride out or face being blasted out the saddle.'

That macabre smile that had so terrified Charlotte Wetherby still graced the angular profile of the infamous gunman. 'Now that ain't a very friendly greeting, marshal,' Hogget scoffed, drawing his mount to a halt. 'All I want is a drink and here you are issuing threats to an innocent traveller.' He nudged the horse closer, clicking his tongue in mock admonition.

'Stay right there!' came the blunt command. 'You and that boss of your'n ain't gonna force innocent settlers from their land. I've received a complaint that you've been threatening folks, so I'm giving you fair warning. Ride out of here now and leave the territory, or I'll be forced to place you under arrest.'

'You've gotten me all wrong, marshal.' Hogget held up his hands ostensibly to show he harboured no grudges. 'Somebody round here has made a mistake. But if'n you want me to leave, then I will. Nobody can say that Bill Hogget goes looking for trouble.' And with that he swung his horse around and trotted back along the street, disappearing around the first bend.

Lincoln frowned. He couldn't believe his luck. Surely it wasn't going to be that easy. A moment of reflection followed before he turned to walk back to the jailhouse. That was when the thunder of hoofs impinged on his ruminations. Rowdy Bill hammered back round the bend, reins clutched in his teeth, a six-shooter in either hand. The startled lawman stood frozen to the spot, the shotgun hanging limply by his side.

It was Deputy Longbaugh who now had to intervene if his boss was not to be gunned down. Wes had suspected some devious skulduggery was being formulated in Rowdy Bill's twisted mind when he gave in too easily. As a result he had stepped onto the veranda to give covering fire should it be needed. Hogget was able to loose off a couple of shots before Wes could make his presence felt. One of them struck Lincoln in the shoulder. He went down. A scream from Kay Lincoln, who was standing behind Wes, soured his aim as he retaliated. The bullets missed the charging bushwhacker but one brought down his horse.

Hogget scrambled to his feet and disappeared down a passage separating the Hardacre Furniture Store from a bootmaker's.

Wes bit his lip, holding back a lurid epithet. 'Get back inside!' he shouted at Kay. 'There's gonna be a lot more lead flying before this business is over and I don't want anyone else in the firing line.'

But the girl was not to be browbeaten. 'Not before I get Pa inside,' she retorted, running into the street. Griff Teale had emerged from the Broken Bottle when the shooting started. He immediately ran across and helped her manhandle the bleeding lawman back into his office.

Wes didn't wait to see how badly the marshal was injured. He ran across to the passage and peered carefully into the gloomy portal. A small animated face appeared at an upstairs window. It was Tommy Hardacre, who had been watching the action with bated breath. 'Hey, Wes!' he called down. The deputy looked up somewhat surprised. 'He headed down towards the livery stable. My bet is he'll make a stand there.' He pointed to a large barn and corral behind the main street. 'Watch yourself. That guy is pure poison.'

Wes smiled to himself. 'I sure will, Tommy,' he replied. 'And much obliged for the warning. I'll remember what you said.' Tommy's face lit up. Praise from a top gun hand like Wes Longbaugh was better than ice cream on Sunday.

With the kid's cogent warning to guide him, Wes edged his way along to the end of the passage. There across a piece of open ground stood the barn with its open door. Nobody was in sight but Wes knew that his every move from here on would be under close observation from the ruthless Hogget. He paused, narrowing his gaze and scanning the wooden structure to tease out any movement. Nothing. It was no use staying where he was, so he made a dash for a stack of hay bales beside the corral.

Immediately the deep chopping roar of a Winchester blasted the silence apart. Only Wes's fleeting move saved him as the bullet ploughed into the sand inches from his boot heels. That was a close call. A silent curse followed that he had failed to bring his own long gun. This was the second time he had made such a vital error. Was he losing his touch? No time to consider such imponderables now.

He would need to get close in to nullify the use of a rifle. That meant getting inside the stable. He had spotted the puff of smoke from an opening in the hay loft, so now he at least knew the location of his quarry. Warily he scrambled along the edge of the corral fence, hidden from view by the angle of uprights. Hogget pumped off a couple of shots that merely chewed lumps of wood from the beams.

As he neared the stable wall, Wes snapped off a round to keep the guy's head down. Then he scuttled inside the building, flattening himself against the wall beside the end stall. The gunfire had unnerved the horses that were becoming restive, stamping their hoofs in terror. Of the ostler there was no sign. He had clearly sought safety elsewhere.

Spotting any movement inside the gloomy interior was difficult. Ensconced in the hay loft, the gunman held the higher ground. A handy ladder close by should effectively neutralize that advantage. Gun pointing upward, Wes gingerly ascended the ladder. He was halfway up when two bullets clipped the edge of the riser.

'Ha, ha, ha!' a ghoulish bout of cackling found Wes tumbling back into the stall. Luckily his fall was broken by the hay. 'I could have had you there, Longbaugh,' the morbid voice called out from somewhere in the dimness of the barn. 'But I like it this way. Makes me feel like a spitting cat tracking a feeble mouse.' Another bout of chilling laughter broke out. 'So come on, hotshot. Let's see how good you are at the stalking game. I always relished that kind of hunting when I was a kid, but it's much more interesting when the prey is human don't you think? And extra special when a guy of your reputation is the reward at the end.'

Wes didn't reply. Keeping close to the ground, he crawled back to the open door. A sudden lunge and he was outside. Two bullets chipped the woodwork close to his head as another bolt of laughter chased him out of sight. Air was sucked into a thudding chest to settle his jangled nerves. The realization struck home that in Rowdy Bill Hogget he was up against a worthy if deadly opponent.

The guy had been right. This was going to be a duel to the finish. A hand absent-mindedly stroked the watch given him by Mace Farlow.

THIRTEEN

. . . AND
RESURRECTED!

Not wishing to be caught out in the open, Wes kept close to the wall, scurrying along round to the far side. A quick peek around the corner of this open doorway found him taking a flying leap into the nearest stall, which luckily was devoid of an equine occupant. The noise could not be avoided. 'Glad to see you've accepted the challenge, Wes,' came the chilling acknowledgement from somewhere in the dim recesses of the stable. 'Now we can get down to business. And may the best man win. Me in this case.'

More spine-tingling hilarity was followed by silence as both men waited for the other to make a move. Over the next half hour, the deadly cat and mouse contest was pursued by both participants in earnest. Gunfire was exchanged, with Hogget

141

becoming ever more irritated as time passed.

The spitting cat's initial macabre sense of fun soon dissolved into an urgent need to get this finished. The comments exchanged between the two gladiators altered perceptibly, with Wes's calm manner becoming more pronounced as his confidence grew. It was a deliberate ploy to annoy his opponent and make him careless. Hogget was well aware that the longer this stalemate dragged on the more likely his adversary was to emerge victorious.

Accordingly, he made the suggestion that this irrational state of affairs could not go on indefinitely. 'This ain't going nowhere, Wes,' he called out from the gloomy interior. 'What say we call it a draw. I'll ride out of here and not look back until I'm over the border back in Utah. I'm sure you can handle Devine on your own without me sticking in your craw. Maybe we'll meet up again someplace and finish this off once and for all. What d'yuh reckon?'

Hogget waited anxiously to hear his opponent's verdict. Saw Tooth held its collective breath while Wes deliberated. When the response came, the answer was not what Hogget had expected, in fact anything but. 'I can't allow you to ride away,' he said in a flat tone devoid of expression making it all the more chilling. 'This became personal when you double-crossed a friend of mine. When he died, I pledged to give up this life for good. But coming up against you has brought the whole business back into focus.'

'What in thunderation you talking about?' was the

impatient reply. 'Who in hell is this mysterious critter I'm supposed to have betrayed?'

Wes struggled to keep his voice steady as the sorry tale related by his old buddy was resurrected. 'Remember Goliath's Stack in the Humboldt Sink?' Wes could almost visualize the startled, horrified look on Hogget's face. 'You should do seeing as it was you that did the dirty on Juno Macklin and his boys.'

The narration suddenly assumed a brittle tone of accusation. 'What you didn't count on was one of the outlaws surviving the ambush. I found him wandering in the desert.' He paused to add gravitas to the denouement. 'Mace Farlow pledged to run you to earth one day. Unfortunately he can't be here for the pay-off, so I'm his substitute. Are you man enough to do the honourable thing? Guess you know exactly what I mean.'

After mulling over his options, Hogget realized he was stuck between a rock and hard place with little room for manoeuvre. The stalking ploy had rebounded on him. That said, he was confident that in such a shoot-out he could outdraw any gunslinger in the south-west. And with Wes Longbaugh's scalp hanging on his belt, Bill Hogget would be cock of the walk. 'You got yourself a deal, Wes. So how we gonna play this?' he called out, feeling upbeat.

'We come out the doors on opposite sides of the stable into the corral,' Wes said. 'Both hands raised so there will be no temptation to pull a fast one. Agreed?' A grunted response found him adding, 'Then we can decide on a fair contest.'

Each of the combatants kept the other under close observation as they emerged warily from cover, sidling out into the open sandy tract of the fenced corral. An enduring ritual of settling scores was about to be re-enacted, one that the gladiators of ancient Rome had perfected for the bloodthirsty pleasure of the Emperor. Later it had been passed down through the ages in various forms until arriving at this current stand-off favoured by western gun-slingers.

'So how we gonna make this a fair fight?' Hogget enquired, flexing his hands and squaring his shoulders to ease out the inevitable tension.

'There's a meadow lark sitting on the fence over yonder watching us,' Wes announced. 'Soon as he lifts off, we go to shooting.'

Hogget nodded. 'Just so long as he don't sit there all day. I ain't the most patient of guys.'

'It won't be long,' Wes replied. 'There's a cat sneaking across from the barn. A minute at most and that bird will be airborne.' Both pairs of eyes now shifted towards the perched bird that was completely oblivious to the part he was playing in this deadly contest. Numerous other eyes were likewise watching from the safety of windows facing onto the back lot.

A light breeze stirred the soft sand underfoot as the feline stalker began its own lethal pursuit. Closer and closer it crawled, all the while its slit eyes never leaving the unwary flyer. The cat stopped at the corner of the stable. Its whole body arched ready for the final dash. An open mouth revealed gleaming white fangs dripping saliva. Both men tensed, sensing the point of no return had been reached.

The cat lunged. At same time the instinct for survival kicked in and the bird rose from its perch.

Both men slapped leather at one and the same moment, but it was Hogget who had that vital edge, that one second separating life from death. His gun blasted. A streak of orange flame and white smoke preceded the chunk of hot lead that raced towards its target. Wes had his own gun out, a thumb drawing back the hammer when the bullet struck him full in the chest. He went down.

A cry of triumph erupted from Hogget's open mouth. Black soulless eyes glinted with the craze-induced power of victory. The strike of the bullet had hit Wes like a steam hammer, yet somehow he was still alive. A hand clawed at his chest. There was a sharp pain but no blood. His bemused brain could not unravel the meaning of this miraculous reprieve from certain death. Then it touched the pocket watch, a finger probing the dent in the tough metal of the casing, and he knew.

His old buddy had offered him a second chance, but fortune such as this had to be grabbed. Already Hogget was sensing that his shot had somehow failed to achieve its lethal purpose. The thumb snapped back, finger tightening on the trigger for a second attempt. But this time he was not quick enough. Wes managed to trigger off two shots, both finding their mark. Blood spouted from Hogget's neck and chest. It was a killing response.

Wes staggered to his feet. A free hand supported bruised ribs as he lurched across to the dying gunman. And there he stood over his adversary, gun aimed low in case he was playing possum. 'No need for another round, Wes,' the dying man groaned. 'We both know I'm done for. But what happened? Sure as eggs is eggs, I had you, didn't I?'

Reaching into his pocket, Wes's face creased up as he withdrew the shattered timepiece. 'Mace had his revenge after all, fella. He gave me this at the end just before he passed on. It was the only thing of value you left him.'

Hogget's eyes bulged. 'Luck just wasn't with me today,' he gasped out, struggling to drag air into a punctured lung. 'Guess I did get my just deserts in the end.' Then a weak smile creased the ashen face as death rattled his cage. 'But at least I can go join Old Nick knowing I was faster on the draw than the great Wes Longbaugh.' A last convulsion, then the blood-filled eyes rolled up and he lay still.

Wes nodded. 'Not that it did you any good.' Then he peered up towards the firmament where the sun had just slid from behind a dark cloud. 'But it sure made me realize you were right all along, Mace. There's always gonna be someone faster on the draw.' He stood there, the Colt Peacemaker hanging by his side. All around silent watchers began to appear. Drawn like moths to the flame of violent death, they gathered round to stare at the morbid sight.

Kay pushed through the prying voyeurs. A hand

146

touched his arm, attempting to break the spell of still being alive. 'I thought that was it when you went down,' she whispered, looking up into his eyes searching for an explanation to the mystery. There was no reaction. It was as if he not heard. A haunted look fastened onto the corpse.

Killing did not come easy, even to a man of Wes Longbaugh's wide experience in that regard. Some guys became immune to the taking of life, indifferent, a casual occurrence no worse than shooting a rabid dog. Not Wes. He always took it personally, each notch on his gun butt shedding a part of his being. That had become especially significant since his encounter with Mace Farlow.

Again Kay shook his arm quietly, asking the question that everyone was asking. 'What happened to bring about this miracle?'

As if in a dream, he handed over the tangled remnants of his lucky escape. 'It would have been me lying there if'n this hadn't come to my rescue.' A tentative hand felt his rib cage, eliciting a grimace of pain. 'It was more than luck that helped me out today. And if'n it's taught me one thing, it's that gunfighting is a mug's game. I'm done with it.'

But abandoning the gun is easier said than done, as Wes had already discovered before even he reached Saw Tooth. And that truth was about to be tested by the intervention of an unexpected arrival.

FOURTEEN

STRENGTH IN NUMBERS

Woollie Buck Rankin had visited the marshal's office, but it was empty. The gunfire behind the line of stores had drawn him to the source of conflict like all the others. Seeing Bill Hogget lying on the ground shook him to the core. He harboured no sympathy for the dead gunman. Those that live by the gun, die by it. Perhaps with Hogget out of the picture, his task would be easier to accomplish. After all, he was here to issue a warning.

That morning the boss had instructed all the hands to assemble outside the main house. He had an important announcement to make. 'We're heading into Saw Tooth to deliver an ultimatum,' he growled out, a grim scowl auguring badly for those on the receiving end.

148

Hard eyes panned across the gathering, which included regular cow hands together with the recent incomers hired solely for their gunfighting ability. The boss was deadly serious. Gone was the natty store-bought suit and frilled white shirt. In their place Devine had clad himself in the customary range gear he wore at round-up time. Around his waist hung a tooled leather gunbelt holding a nickel-plated Merwin and Hulbert .44 revolver – a worthy competitor to the Colt .45.

'I've had enough of these sodbusters coming into the San Miguel and sectioning off land that rightly belongs to me,' Devine snapped. 'This is the time for you guys to earn the extra dough I'm paying you.' He paused, drawing on the cigar clutched between his teeth. 'So we're going to fence off the whole valley tomorrow. Anybody still there will be shot on sight. Be ready to ride in half an hour.'

Rankin had been standing at the back. He had expected this. The signs had been there every since those bull-headed nesters led by Sam Wetherby had banded together to protect their adjudged rights. Nevertheless, it came as a shock that his boss was actually prepared to start a range war to achieve his callous ambition of land grabbing. The foreman reckoned he had turned a blind eye to the way things were heading for long enough. This was one step too far. For the major's own sake he needed to be stopped and made to see reason. Unbridled aspirations of supremacy had soured any rational judgement. Something had to be done.

But what could he do on his own? Clearly the legally appointed representatives had to be alerted in order to squash the project before it got out of hand and blood was spilled. He hung back, waiting until the corral had emptied before hurrying across to where his horse was tethered behind the barn. Secrecy was paramount to avoid being spotted leaving ahead of schedule and arousing suspicions.

A thirty-minute margin would give him chance to circle behind the surrounding hills to join the main trail to Saw Tooth beyond the immediate environs of the ranch buildings. Once out of sight, he pushed his horse to the gallop, urging the mount to its maximum. There was no time to lose if'n the marshal was to be persuaded to organise some form of resistance to the challenge.

As soon as he saw the dead body of Rowdy Bill Hogget, Rankin knew that the chips were down. So the hired gunslinger had gone up against Longbaugh and paid the price. 'I need to speak with you urgently,' he said, standing in front of the dazed deputy. He waited for the new lawman to heed what he had to say. 'Devine is on his way here with all the crew right now to give warning that he intends to wire off the Valley tomorrow.' A gasp went up from the gathered farmers. 'He has to be stopped before it's too late and a war breaks out.'

Wes fixed a sceptical eye onto the cowboy. 'How do I know this isn't some trick to lure us into a trap,' he retorted. 'I seem to recall Devine had planned something similar the other day down by the creek.'

The accusation was supported by numerous grunts, making Rankin feel decidedly nervous, like a lamb caught in a circle of hungry wolves. But he held his nerve. 'Would I be here risking my own skin to warn you if'n it wasn't the danged truth?' the foreman appealed. 'I've been with Major Devine a long time, since the war. At heart he's a good rancher. But he don't like change. And these nesters coming into the valley have rattled him big time. He's a worried man and that makes him dangerous.'

'Under the government-sponsored Homestead Act, we have every right to farm a section of land designated as open range.' It was Sam Wetherby who spoke up, expressing the view shared by all the farmers present. 'And according to the records lodged in the county office at Ridgeway, the San Miguel Valley complies with that ruling. It's a big valley. There's room enough for everybody to prosper if some folks weren't so darned greedy.'

'You try telling that to Devine. He ain't listening no more.' Buck Rankin was genuinely contrite that his boss had adopted this bull-headed attitude. 'He needs confronting. But my fear is that anybody stands in his way will be trampled underfoot.'

'How long before he gets here?' Wes asked, now fully convinced of the cowman's veracity.

'He can't be more than fifteen minutes behind. So you need to act fast.' The urgency of the man's resolve was enough for Wes to issue firm orders. 'You men get over to the Broken Bottle now. But don't do anything without my say so.' The gritty order balked no opposition. None of these men, even the recalcitrant Sam Wetherby, wanted to become involved in a range war. They were ostensibly peaceable farmers.

'Spread yourselves around the room but keep your guns out of sight,' Wes continued, trying to figure out a plan of action on the hoof. 'I'll join you soon as I've seen Miss Lincoln safely back home to tend her wounded father. This ain't no place for a woman until Devine and his crew have had their wings clipped.' His final query was to the edgy foreman of the Star LD. 'You with me in this, Woollie?'

'If'n it means bringing the major to his senses, then count me in.'

Wes was moved by the foreman's candour. Going against the grain for the sake of a greater good of the community took guts. And this guy had bucketfuls. Wes was not slow in letting his feelings be known. 'It took great courage for you to come here,' he commended the troubled cowpoke, patting him on the shoulder. 'And I'm figuring your boss will thank you as well once he's been persuaded that only blood and heartache can come out of a range war.'

And with that the deputy urged the men to disperse and gird up their loins for the approaching confrontation. On the walk back to her house, Wes encouraged Kay to stay with her father. 'I don't want you getting involved in something that might turn nasty.' He peered deep into her eyes. 'There's nothing going on between me and Maria,' he insisted. 'She was only showing me the bruises on her shoulder where Devine manhandled her. She had run away and I was the only one who could help her. I couldn't turn her away, could I?' Soulful eyes implored the girl to believe him.

A softer more engaging look found Kay gripping his arm. 'I realize now that I jumped to the wrong conclusions. That was wrong of me. Can we start again?' Wes responded by placing an arm around her shoulder and smiling as they hurried down the street. But he could not ignore that a fresh start depended on how the imminent showdown panned out.

The atmosphere in the Broken Bottle was thick with suppressed tension. Wes felt it like a slap in the face as he pushed open the batwing doors. 'Don't look so stiff and jumpy,' he exhorted. 'We don't want Devine smelling a rat. And remember, when they come through that door, don't make a move to disarm them until I give the word. I'll only step in to arrest him if'n he refuses to back down. We can only hope and pray that he sees sense. But it's a long shot, as I'm sure you're all aware.'

The men grimly nodded their understanding. Moments later the thud of approaching horses saw the men visibly stiffen. Anxious looks passed between them. Hands tightened around old firearms that had seen better days. Sweat broke out on more than one forehead as men breathed deep to calm their jangling nerves. A stamping of boots on the boardwalk outside and the door was thrown open.

Leroy Devine strutted, in followed by a dozen

hands all carrying guns. The regular cowboys looked decidedly nervous. They were easily distinguishable from the hired gunslingers, for whom this was their bread and butter. Devine stumped over to the bar and grabbed hold of the nearest bottle of whiskey. Raising it to his lips, he knocked back a generous slug. 'I see all the troublemakers are present,' he commented acidly, looking around and aiming a blunt grimace at Griff Teale. 'Just as well 'cos I'm here to inform you all that as of tomorrow noon, your land is forfeit, confiscated by the Star LD Cattle Raising Company.'

'You can't do that, it ain't legal,' shouted Sam Wetherby, stepping forward. 'We have official permission to farm land under the Home. . . .'

He never got to finish. 'I'm making the law around here now. And I say this is cattle country. No sodbusters allowed. Any still around when we begin wiring off the valley will be shot on sight for trespassing.'

That was the moment Wes made his presence felt. 'If'n you thought that Rowdy Bill Hogget could come here and get rid of the marshal and me, you've been badly misinformed. We're both still in business. It's Hogget who is in need of an undertaker. Ain't that right, boys?' Snarled grunts of agreement hailed this startling declaration. 'There'll be no vigilante law in this county.'

Devine soon recovered his coolness, deriding the remark with a sneering guffaw. 'Hogget may be down, but I've gotten a dozen men here tooled up and ready to blast anybody to Kingdom Come who stands in our way.'

'Think again, Devine.' Wes raised a hand, the signal for all the farmers to jam their weapons into the backs of the nearest opponent. The surprise reversal of fortunes caught them completely off guard. 'Now drop your guns the lot of you, and get out of town fast. And I suggest you leave the county pronto.' He skewered the ringleader with a caustic glower. 'All except you, Mister Devine. I'm holding you in jail until the circuit judge arrives. Then we'll see who manages the law around here.'

Devine gritted his teeth. An angry glare panning across the crowd of nesters came to rest on his foreman. Rankin was holding a gun to the head of one of the hired gunnies. 'So it was you who spilt the beans. I never had you down as a double-crossing Judas, Buck.' His tone appeared to be almost regretful as he moved across to where Rankin was standing near the door. 'After all we've been through together. I make you my right-hand man. How could you let me down like this?'

'I didn't want to, Major. But you forced my hand. You needed to be stopped,' the earnest cowpoke pleaded. 'You lost track of what was right and wrong. Somebody had to make you see the light.'

Devine shook his head in disappointment at the betrayal of a trusted employee. But it was all a sham, a devious ploy to persuade the gathering that he had given up. Then, quick as a striking rattler, he drew a small derringer from his vest pocket and drilled the

155

disloyal foreman in the guts.

'There's only one way of dealing with a wayward cheat.' Close up the small weapon packed a deadly punch. Rankin slid to the floor. He would not be getting up again. And there was still one unused .41 bullet left. Devine swung it to cover the deputy, who had been wrong-footed by the sudden reversal of fate. He backed to the door, 'And remember I still have the Merwin if'n anybody tries to stop me getting away.' He drew the revolver, encouraging those such as Sam Wetherby who were edging forward ready to rush him that such a manoeuvre would be fatal.

Devine knew that his days in San Miguel county were numbered, but if'n he could reach the ranch there was enough dough stashed away in the safe to give him a solid grubstake someplace else.

Wes cursed himself for thinking there was enough support from the farmers to stymie the land-grabber's ruthless objective. The error of judgement had made him over-confident, arrogant even. As such he had left his gun holstered. The consideration as to whether he could draw and get a shot off was nullified when bad luck chose to intervene. Fate is a fickle mistress who decided at that moment to toss a spanner into the works.

After seeing that her father was settled at home, Kay Lincoln had hurried back to the Broken Bottle, her intention being to intervene somehow. How that would be achieved against the might of the Star LD faction had not been contemplated. A woman in love has thoughts only for the man to whom her affections are aimed. Wes Longbaugh was taking on the domineering rancher helped or hindered by a bunch of small-time nesters. And she wanted to be there by his side.

Devine was backing out of the saloon when the girl arrived. He immediately saw his chance and took it, grabbing her roughly and using her as a shield. 'Anybody comes after me and it'll be the girl that suffers,' he snarled as Wes took a step forward. 'That goes especially for you, Longbaugh. I can see by that lovesick gape that Miss Lincoln has captured your heart.' The callous braggart sniggered, keeping the girl between himself and the deputy as he forced Kay onto a horse adjacent to his own. 'We're riding out. I'll let her go on the far side of White Horse Gorge providing you keep your distance.'

Holding the girl's trailing rein, Devine led the way, leaving Wes fuming and impotent to intercede. All he could do was follow at a distance and hope that the callous rancher kept his word. Kay's safety was all that mattered now, but first he instructed Wetherby to disarm the Star LD hands, then escort them to the county line.

An hour's riding found Devine and Kay at a deep gorge that was spanned by a trestle bridge wide enough for a wagon to pass over. Once on the far side, Devine tied Kay to a nearby pine tree where she was in full view. And there he waited for his arch enemy to arrive. He did not have long to wait. In the meantime he had fastened two sticks of dynamite to the main stanchions ready to blow the moment Wes showed any signs of crossing the bridge.

'I knew you wouldn't give up,' Devine called across the yawning gulf. 'Guys like you never know when to quit. I'm gonna blow this bridge to smithereens. It's a half day's ride down river to the next crossing point, more than enough time for me to disappear. So the last laugh is on me, sucker.' He held up the box of matches. 'Get ready to enjoy the fireworks. Don't worry about the girl. She's over yonder out of danger.'

He bent down and was about to light the fuse wire. Suddenly, out of the blue, a figure clad in a red dress ran out from the cover of some rocks. Maria Elena had decided to return to the Star LD after Wes had spurned her advances. Leroy Devine could be a brute at times but where else could she go? The dilemma had been running through her troubled mind when the rancher and his captive had appeared. Seeing how he manhandled the poor girl had brought all her hatred for the man rushing to the fore.

In a flash she saw her opportunity. The rancher always carried the key to his private safe on his person. The plan to make him pay for her suffering at his hands was formulated in an instant. Luckily he had his back to her as she rushed out from cover. She grabbed hold of a rock and slammed it hard over Devine's exposed head. The man staggered under the heavy blow, blood pouring from a gash in his scalp. Without any squeamish regret she then pushed him over the edge of the ravine.

Wes saw everything that happened and immediately spurred his horse over the bridge. He took a sobbing Maria Elena in his arms and together they went across to release Kay from her bonds. All three hugged one another panting heavily, overwhelmed by how events could have so easily taken a different turn.

After recovering her composure, Maria explained how she had been heading back to the ranch, but stopped at White Horse Gorge debating with herself whether that was the only option open to her. 'So what do you intend doing now?' Wes asked.

Kay butted in. 'There'll always be a place for you in Saw Tooth,' she enthused, grateful for the girl's intervention on her behalf.

'I thank you, *señorita*,' she said casting a longing eye towards her old flame. 'But I don't think that a good idea.' Then a smile broke across the dark-eyed beauty's face. 'I have other plans now Señor Devine's hold over me has been broken.'

A sly gleam in her eye raised a puzzled frown on Wes's face. 'So what is it you are plotting, Maria?'

'It best I keep that secret,' she smirked, shaking her shoulders in a coquettish gesture. 'But rest assured, Maria is heading for a life of luxury, perhaps in California.' And with that she bade them *adios* with a spritely wave and disappeared into the rocks, moments later appearing on her horse heading towards Star LD land.

'Now I wonder what she has in mind?' the deputy remarked, scratching his head.

'Whatever it is, she appears to have it in hand,' came the upbeat reply. 'We have to decide how Wes Longbaugh is going to spend his time now that he can finally hang up those guns.'

'I can think of one thing straight away,' he said taking her in his arms. Somewhere across the great beyond, an old gunfighter casually smiled and nodded his head. At least his life had not been wasted after all.